SEIZED BY THE MAFIA KING

EVIE ROSE

Copyright © 2025 by Evie Rose

All rights reserved.

No part of this book may be reproduced in any form or by any electronic or mechanical means, including information storage and retrieval systems, without written permission from the author, except for the use of brief quotations in a book review.

This story is a work of fiction. Names, characters, places, and incidents are the product of the author's imagination or are used fictitiously. Any resemblance to actual events, locales, or persons, living or dead, is coincidental.

Cover: © 2025 by Evie Rose. Images under licence from Deposit Photos.

❦ Created with Vellum

1

WILLOW

If I were rating this wedding, it would be two stars. It gets an extra star because the church is nice, and the guests are well-presented and on time. But ideally, it needs starting again, with my choice of groom. And dress.

And shoes I can walk in.

Honestly, I'd prefer to put my whole life back on the shelf and try another one, like it was a book. As it turns out, being born into the Maldon mafia is overrated. It says something when my best option is an arranged marriage to Witham, a mafia boss who practically has that creepy-scare music around him.

I control my breathing as the priest drones on about the sanctity of the union, but the panic keeps rising. This is my *life*, and I can't restart it.

I glance to the side. My future husband is about sixty, with a gut and a grubby blond moustache and beady little eyes.

He looks back at me, missing my face altogether and focussing on my breasts. His gaze is a slick of black, gritty oil over my body.

This monster will *own* me.

Fear seeps in like damp into a paperback book. I'm too old for his tastes, I know that, and I've got a plan. But what if it doesn't work?

It will. It has to.

Out of the corner of my eye I regard my family seated in the church behind me. My three brothers and my mother, and various uncles and aunts. They're impassive. Uncaring. I'm just a stupid little girl to them, only useful to be traded off.

When I said to my brother Liam about wanting to work in a bookshop, he sneered that Maldons don't fetch and *carry*, so I've never told anyone else about my dream. I build the bookshop in my mind, planning my sections and my stock. When everything is bad, it's my happy place. A warm comfort blanket.

Usually.

Today, it won't appear. I try to think of rows of my favourite author's books, but all I can see is the priest, the gold cross and the altar and the marble on the floor, and the sinister, greasy presence of my fiancé.

I have the phone number of the contact memorised, and the internet rumours are that the London Mafia Syndicate are uncompromising towards the sordid trade Witham does. Once I'm married, I can give the tip-off, and escape in the chaos that ensues. Witham won't be expecting it, not like my family, who remember how I called the police on them when I was twelve, and have viewed me as a traitor ever since.

Me and my big mouth, my mother said when she saw the bruises afterwards.

I didn't know that my family owned all the police in the area, and my lesson healed into an instinct never to risk being caught in an escape again. But my family doesn't own the London Mafia Syndicate. They will get bloody revenge for Witham's *tastes*. The same stuff my family turns a blind eye to because they want Witham's territory.

Even so, an animal fear rises in me. Everywhere I look there's trouble or judgement, or no way out. The church door is too far away, I'd never make it before my brothers caught me and frogmarched me back.

I'm trapped.

For my plan to work, I need to be married to Witham, but even so, I can't help but pray to any god that might be listening, or something, anything. I have this rock in my gut. I don't want this marriage.

"Does anyone here present know of any good reason—"

I see the door open before the crash of wood against stone hits my ears and draws shrieks from several of my aunts as a man strolls into the church followed by a dozen men with very large guns. All pointing at my family, my fiancé's family, and *me*.

"I didn't get my invitation," the man drawls, and my heart unexpectedly patters. Not in a fearful way, nope. In a thrilled way. Because the intruder's voice is like caramel and brandy cream, smooth and dark and utterly decadent, with a dangerous kick.

This man exudes casual power. He's wearing a blue-black suit, with a tie the colour of a winter ocean. His crisp white shirt is impeccable, as though he really is a guest at a wedding.

"I told you there would be consequences, Witham." The man paces up the aisle, his hands in his pockets.

He isn't even armed. Or rather, he doesn't have his gun drawn. That's not needed, since he has effortlessly outmanoeuvred my family and the Withams.

As he gets closer, I take him in. He's tall. Maybe six-foot-six? His hair is the deepest brown, almost black, and he has deliberately careless stubble that makes him even more masculine, as though his wide shoulders and pronounced Adam's apple didn't already.

He comes to a stop and stares at me, pale blue eyes wide like he's seen a ghost. We regard each other for a long moment, and I know it's crazy, but there's recognition unlike anything I've ever felt. He sees *me*. Not a bride, not a Maldon princess. Not a sister or a daughter. Not even just a passably pretty girl who happens to be in his way. He reaches into my body and weighs my soul in his palm.

And it's the same for me. Objectively, he's a terrifying and gorgeous man who could kill me and everyone in this room with a flick of his elegant fingers. But I can see a spark of humour in his eyes, a mouth that could be quick to smile, and a gentleness to his power, hidden beneath that sharp suit and arrogant jawline.

Compared to my betrothed, he's... Well. There's no comparison.

"I'm sorry," Witham begins.

The eyes of the man standing regarding me go icy.

"Bethnal." My brother's voice holds a note of fear. "Why are you here?"

Ohhhh sugar. As in Bethnal Green in London? It sounds like it's a leafy paradise, but Bethnal Green is in the East End, and notorious for being the cut-throat part of London. I didn't dare try to get the phone number of *Bethnal*.

Witham gulps. "I'm sure we can come to some—"

"You haven't been paying your debts, Witham. Do the Maldons know that?"

I glance at my eldest brother, and no, clearly he did not.

"Three months, you owe me," the Bethnal kingpin continues, wandering around the front of the church as though he owns the place. "I've been very patient, and the interest is accruing rapidly."

He picks up the sacramental wine from the altar and the priest makes a strangled sound of protest. Bethnal sniffs, wrinkles his lip and sets it back down. His meaning is clear. It's not even good enough for him to bother desecrating.

"Then we found the *children*." The distaste in Bethnal's expression flares into disgust. "And I thought, why should a man be getting married today, when he was profiting from *that*, and failing to pay his debts?"

The air is sucked from the room as there's an audible intake of breath.

My head spins.

His words are low and harsh. He's furious.

And he's removed my one hope of escape.

"You owe me money, Witham. And you're going to pay. Now."

"I will," Witham stutters. "I just need a bit more time. Next week."

There's cold silence, and I freeze in it. Bethnal has already dealt with Witham's child trafficking, so there's nothing for me to report now. There will be no scramble to send out his men, or confusion at the announcement of the attack. It was all finished while we prepared for the wedding, and I've got nothing but an angry future husband.

Fate, this is a terrible mistake.

He'll take it out on me.

Being trapped, married to a mafia boss, isn't supposed to be my life. Fear creeps into my skin with a stench of rotting dreams.

"Tomorrow!" Witham trembles next to me and glances

at my brother Robert, who he negotiated all this with since he's the Maldon kingpin.

Robert nods. "I'll get it to you tomorrow."

The last of my hope dies. It's not like I really thought my family cared about who they're giving me to, but it still hurts that this is Robert's response. He'd rather the deal went ahead, even if it's now public knowledge he's marrying me to a monster.

Instinctively, I take a small step away from Witham. It's no more than a noiseless slide, but it draws Bethnal's gaze again. He scans my face, then lounges against the altar and turns his attention to Robert.

"You're going to let her marry this piece of shit?" he asks no one in particular.

"You'll have your money before nine," Robert replies.

His words fall on my shoulders, sinking down as though he's piled lead into my veins. My brother has priorities, and it's not me.

"No." Bethnal narrows his eyes, then seamlessly pulls out a gun and shoots Witham in the head. He falls to the floor with a thud.

I jerk backwards, gaping in horror at the blood splattered on the smooth marble and sprayed over my white dress.

Someone in the congregation screams, and there's mutterings.

He's dead.

The man who was supposed to be my husband is now a corpse.

My heart hammers. Am I saved from this marriage after all? But my god, is that even the word? I'll have to go back to my family. Since the arranged marriage hasn't happened as Robert wanted, will he insist I have the usual Essex Cartel virgin auction? And Robert is going to be angry. I can already see it in the set of his jaw.

"I'll have the Witham territory as partial payment of his debts. And to make up the rest, I'll be taking this," Bethnal says as he holsters his gun.

What? The gun?

Bethnal approaches me and bows, and for a second, I think that's it. Then I'm over his shoulder and a shriek escapes me. I shove at his back and squirm as he carries me, and I bump with each quick step. I kick my feet, but I'm really high, and he holds me tight. So, so tight.

I look up at my brothers' furious faces and Bethnal's men neatly backing out of the church. No one is lifting a finger to rescue me.

Bethnal steals me away.

I'm not getting married. I'm saved from a marriage that might have been worse than death and this is an opportunity. A chance to escape to a new life.

Because it hits me. I'm being kidnapped.

2

ZANE

"Turner, plan B," I tell my second-in-command on the phone. My captive girl sits next to me in the armoured SUV as we head away from the church faster than is advisable or legal.

Turner swears colourfully.

"I know," I reply. "You'll get a pay rise."

"I don't want to take over that shitshow," Turner grumbles. "What happened to ruining the wedding, reminding Witham who he was beholden to, and ensuring there wasn't anything too grubby about the marriage?"

What indeed? All that exploded when I saw Witham's bride, and a creature inside of me went berserk.

She's mine. I have to have her, whatever the cost.

"The plan changed. Deal with it." Turner will. He was as horrified as I was at what we discovered this morning, and has been loyal to me since before I took over Bethnal Green.

I hang up and regard the girl I just kidnapped. She's gorgeous. Her body is slender, and the white silk hugs her curves. Her long brown hair has a slight wave that gives it movement and life. But it's her face that captivates me in a way I can't begin to explain. She's perfect.

My heart rate won't lower. My cock is solid.

I have never responded to anyone like this before. I'm one of the grumpiest and most violent members of the London Mafia Syndicate, but I don't abduct women.

And neither do I fall in love.

Never, in fact. I thought I was immune, or incapable.

"Wedding crashers usually just drink the booze, you know that, right?" she says, smoothing her dress over her knees, and glancing around the car nervously. She's remarkably calm, all things considered, but her pulse in her neck is as frantic as mine.

I have the rash desire to bite her there and feel her heartbeat against my lips. To hold her life between my teeth, and consume her completely. I want to lick her all over then bury my cock in her.

Keeping from mauling her is taking all my strength.

"I took the best thing on offer," I reply instead, and it's true.

Something that should never be mine. She's obviously young and innocent, and quite aside from the fact I'm a London mafia boss and she's a Maldon mafia princess—part of the Essex cartel who regularly cause problems for London—there's the age gap. I'd like to comfort myself that I'm at least not as ancient as her now-dead almost-husband, but it doesn't change anything. I'm too old for her.

"Mmm." She hums sceptically. "I'm glad we didn't stay for speeches. They usually are pretty dull, but Witham's would have been murder."

I give a bark of unexpected laughter, and see our future with her giggling as I tickle her in bed. The image of punishing her for her sassy mouth by pinning her down and thrusting into her hardens my already-rigid cock further.

Her dark-green eyes—the colour of a pine forest at dusk—flit towards me and take me in. I swear her look is so piercing she can tell how much this tie cost and knows how many grey hairs I have to the nearest ten.

"Though, Robert—my eldest brother—had some embarrassing stories in his speech from when I was five, so maybe they would have been almost as entertaining as my abduction."

"I'm glad I saved you from any embarrassment," I reply. And him from death. Humiliate my girl? Abso-fucking-lutely not.

"Thanks. No one is going to hear about that time I puked because I ate too much chocolate. They'll be too busy gossiping about how my butt looked over your shoulder."

The growl that wells up from my chest is feral. They better not have been looking. She's *mine*.

She looks askance at me, and I restrain myself. A bit. I still probably look like a grumpy old bastard, which is nothing more than the reality.

"Why did you kidnap me?" she asks casually.

The answer is complicated and simple. Because I had to. Because I think I fell in love with her at first sight. Because leaving her in that church was out of the question, and anyone who might take her from me remaining alive is unthinkable.

I want long nights with her sweaty and satisfied and asleep in my arms, and I can't accept anything that isn't moving us towards that inevitable end.

"What's your name?" I say instead. My obsession needs every detail about her, and this is a good place to start.

"Willow Maldon."

"Zane Bethnal." Two words she'll get to know well. One as her surname—sooner or later—and the other as the name she'll use to beg for mercy when I'm licking her to orgasm for the fifth time within an hour.

"I know who you are," she replies with a little eye roll. "We do have the internet in Essex."

"What a relief. It's not possible to recognise anyone without it. How old are you?" I'm just torturing myself now.

"Twenty."

Damn. She's a baby, and I'm a full twenty-two years older than her. Old enough to be her father, and while young, sweet women have never been my preference before, Willow is different. I simultaneously long to protect her and use her beautiful body in filthy, depraved ways that make her writhe and moan and scream my name as she's overcome with pleasure.

She's *twenty*.

And yet... I run my gaze over her again, taking in her curves. She's old enough to make her own decisions. She was getting married, after all. There's no denying the curiosity in the tilt of her head as she waits for me to reciprocate. I don't. I'm loath to admit I'm more than twice her age.

"Where are we going?" she eventually asks, in a light conversational tone, like we've met at a party.

We're almost out of Essex and green fields whiz past. "My estate in Suffolk."

"And then what?"

I bounce you on my cock until you're pregnant? We get married, I fuck you raw, fill you with my come over and over? I treasure and love you and defile you in bed?

I really didn't plan this.

"Am I your hostage now?"

"My guest," I correct her abruptly.

What am I going to do with Willow? My little bunny. It would be better for her if she never knew how I feel.

Maybe I can just keep her, as she says, as my captive. Perhaps that would be enough?

"Kidnapping your guests and carrying them over your shoulder is normal in London?"

I sigh.

"Because it feels more like I'm a deposit to ensure my brother pays up for the Witham territory," she continues when I don't respond.

And that's when it hits me that though I've given this girl my heart, she doesn't know me. Yet.

"I don't need your brother's money. I have plenty."

"So why were you at the wedding, demanding payment?"

As it turned out, I was at the wedding to have my entire world rearranged by meeting my soulmate.

But I didn't realise that until later. I told myself it was to ruin Witham's nuptials and ensure he paid, but it wasn't that either. It was because I couldn't accept that shithead continuing to live after I saw what he'd done.

Despite my well-earned reputation for ruthlessness, it was an inconvenient sense of justice that brought me to her wedding, drew me to working with the London Mafia Syndicate, and even makes me play along with their absurd "maths" games. I walked out of an emergency meeting of the London Mafia Syndicate to be here. Admittedly, I would probably have left anyway, because although I now understand why a mafia boss would do something so stupid as pretend the Syndicate was a maths club to protect his wife from the truth, I'm better at killing than mental arithmetic and spreadsheets.

"I dislike the hurting of innocents," I say eventually.

I saw far too much of that as a kid in the care system. I was lucky that the kingpin of Bethnal noticed me, and took me in. But that wasn't the case for many, many others.

"Again, interesting logic, Bethnal. Is ruining my wedding not hurting me?"

"Not compared to going through with it."

"Until I get home," she mutters under her breath.

That's better left unacknowledged, because will I let her go? I'm not sure I can.

"What would you usually be doing on a weekday morning?" I ask instead.

"Reading." She shrugs. "Not many options available given my family," she adds defensively.

"What's your favourite book?" I need to know everything about Willow, and this is a good place to start: with a hobby she likes.

"There's a mafia story I really like. The heroine is kidnapped by an enemy, and then he *lets her go.*" Her gaze is fixed on the window, gazing out.

"That doesn't sound exciting."

Willow raises her eyebrows. "It's a great ending for everyone."

Not the ending I want for our story.

"I'm not much of a reader myself. I might skip that one. Unless it's in audio?" I take her very literally to see what she comes back with.

"It's a live-action movie," she says tartly. "Complete with very realistic special effects."

I smother a laugh. "Realistic huh. Do they include the part where she falls for her captor and he makes her come repeatedly, until she begs him to stop because it's too good?"

"No. That bit got *cut* out."

"Edited. What a pity. It was in the book then." God this is fun. I don't think I've ever enjoyed a woman's company so much. "They always say the book is better than the movie. This proves it."

Maybe despite our differences we can work this out...

I relax slightly as we turn past the gatehouse into my estate and make our way through the woods, along the twisting drive that leads to the house. We've found some common ground—she loves books and I'm willing to try whatever will please her—and we're back safe in my territory.

"You know," she continues thoughtfully, toying with one ugly ivory white shoe. "I was looking forward to the cake."

"You like cake?"

She glances casually out of the window and slides the shoes off, revealing perfect little feet. Good to see she's getting comfortable, and I'm glad I carried her from the church because they look like torture devices. Maybe she'd lend them to Turner.

"Who doesn't like cake?" she replies.

"I can take it or leave it." I'd rather eat her. "I'll get you more cake."

"Oh, thanks." She looks into my eyes, and behind the light chatter, there's something else that I can't identify. "Lemon drizzle is my favourite."

"I'll have the chef—"

She grabs the handle, shoves the door open, and before I realise what she's doing and grab for her, she's dived out of the moving car. Fear surges through me as she rolls on the grassy bank.

Shit. What if she's hurt?

"Stop!" I yell and bash my fist on the obscured glass between me and the driver.

We screech to a halt that jerks me forward, and I scramble after her, out of the car, just quick enough to see her white dress streaming behind her as she sprints into the woods. She's lifted it so it doesn't trip her, and I catch a tantalising glimpse of delicate ankles.

My heart thuds not for panic, but for life. She's okay, and my relief at seeing her unharmed is so intense it's like someone rewound time on a shooting.

I stare after her. My little bunny can *run*. She's trying to escape. She's clever, and fuck, she's so *brave*. I admire that as much as the beautiful wrapping.

Did I just fall for her even more? That dignity in the church as my men walked in armed to the teeth to wreck her wedding, and when her unworthy fiancé was shot right beside her. Her humour and her fearlessness. She's remarkable.

I should let her go. It would be consistent with all those fine thoughts about how I'm too old for her, and she's too good for me. But my ideals are gone in the reality of her absence. Even after mere seconds, I can feel the empty sensation of being in a glass jar descending again.

I've waited forty-two years to find her. I'm never giving her up.

She wants a chase?

I'll catch her.

3

WILLOW

I crash through the forest, cursing my stupid shoes, and the necessity of bare feet. Why-oh-why did I wear heels to the wedding?

At least the leaves are deep and cushioned as I sprint away from the man who took me. I hold the train of my dress in one hand, and my hair whips over my shoulders and drags behind, the air caressing my nape. The sun is dappled through the trees. It's not even dark. I don't have any advantage other than the surprise of my escape.

But this is my only chance, and I'm going to take it.

I run, forcing my legs to move faster than they want to, the muscles burning already. Damn cardio. I drag in breaths, open-mouthed, and run with a single focus: freedom.

The plan to escape Witham might have worked, but Bethnal? A London Mafia Boss? That's a whole different, more dangerous, thing.

Besides, I'm just a girl. I'm of no use to someone like Zane Bethnal.

I don't think he'll even chase—

"I'm coming for you, little bunny." Zane's voice bounces around the forest, making it seem like he's everywhere. It's eerie, despite the sunny day.

My heart thuds in my chest as my legs channel the fear that pulses from my heart. I cannot be trapped again. I weave through the trees, searching for something that might help. Could I climb a tree? No. Is there a house nearby where I can plead for help? No.

I curse that I didn't get out earlier, but this small, winding road was the first time the car slowed down enough for me to have the guts to do it.

Faster. I have to be quicker and smarter than the mafia boss.

My body isn't used to this and every part of it is screaming for me to stop. It hurts. My legs, my feet, my lungs, my heart.

Even my treacherous mind whispers, *Why go to this effort to get away from a man as sexy as Zane Bethnal? It's futile. He's taller and stronger than you. He can take one step for two of yours. He'll catch you if he wants to.*

No.

I have to keep going. For once, I have a chance. I have the element of surprise.

All I've ever known is being constrained and told that what I wanted wasn't important. Smacked down if I tried to express an opinion, and punished for doing what I thought was right. Everyone in my family thinks working in a shop is beneath a Maldon. They'll never think to look for me there, if I can just escape Bethnal, I could make a new life with the money I have in a secret account.

Footsteps thud, heavy and determined, behind me.

Oh sugar. I snake through the trees, and pain from my feet shoots up my nerves. My arms pump and my legs are jelly-ish as I try to get to some unknown safe place.

The trees are endless.

And that's when I hear his breathing, almost as loud as my own harsh panting and the pounding of my heart.

He's really chasing me. Like he means it.

"Help!" I yell the word into the forest, and my panic makes it a screech. "Help!"

An animal skitters off into the undergrowth, and then it's just the yellow sunlight, the green of the canopy above, the smooth tree trunks, and my path through the endless crunch of leaves. The land has begun to rise, and my limbs are getting tired. My chest burns. I'm slowing, despite everything.

What if he catches me, what will he do…?

He'll make good on what he said in the car. Cake, and making his captive come until she begs him to stop because it's too good. And then a worse thought snatches at my ankle, dragging at me like a ball and chain.

What if he doesn't catch me?

What if I never find out all the ways he'd be filthy and terrifying and so, so hot.

I want him to catch me and do things to me, but I shouldn't.

"There's no one else here, bunny," he rasps, and it's not even a shout. "There's no escape."

A sob escapes me at how close he is, and how alone we are.

There's empty woodland for miles. I was an idiot to think I could get out. He's a massive, powerful, muscled kingpin, and I'm a twenty-year-old girl who doesn't do enough exercise.

Giving a futile burst of speed, I push my body to the painful limits.

I jerk as he grabs my upper arm and spins me around, shoving me against a tree. I let out an "oof" as my back hits the trunk, but it's not enough to hurt. Or maybe it is, and I can't feel it past the terror rising in my throat.

Raising my hands, I instinctively go to strike at his face. His eyes. To scratch and claw and get away again, but he's too quick. He grabs one wrist then the other in a punishing grip and forces them above my head.

He's breathing heavily, but not fast, and his ice-blue eyes bore into me.

Scowling up at him—and it is up since he's so tall—there's a mess of emotions in my heaving chest and we stare at each other for long seconds as I drag in oxygen like I've been underwater my whole life.

He doesn't move, just keeping me pinned, and not saying anything. I don't know what to do. Cry? Try to knee him in the crotch? I have a feeling he'll anticipate any attack I make.

The worst thing? He hardly has a hair out of place, while I'm sure I'm a red, blotchy, sweaty mess. He's utterly gorgeous, and has chased me in a suit. He's discarded his jacket and tie, and undone his top button, but his shirt remains tucked into his trousers neatly and he's not even panting.

The tension ratchets up between us as my breathing evens out, but he doesn't hit me like Robert would have, or berate me like my mother.

The silence draws out my tension, and I begin to shake.

I should look down and protect my face from the inevitable blow, but I stupidly don't, filled with a fire I haven't felt for years.

"Just get it over with!" I shout, frustration and fear bubbling over.

"What?" he asks, calm and dangerous. "Get *what* over with?"

"Whatever you're going to do," I reply sulkily. I can't stop him.

"I will never hurt you, Willow." His voice goes soft. "And I will kill anyone who does. I will break the bones of anyone who so much as touches you."

That statement steals my breath.

There's no reason to trust him. Except, it feels right.

"Fuck." He tightens his grip on my wrists. "Don't run from me again, little bunny."

I press my lips together, even as my body tingles everywhere we touch, but I'm not making any promises.

He brings his hand to my face, and I flinch away, but I can't get far.

"Willow." The tips of his fingers are as gentle as a summer breeze as he touches my cheek. "Who did this to you?"

Huffing, I shake my head. He's knows. It's obvious. Violence against women is part of the Essex mafias, he should know that. When I was a kid, it was casual cuffs around the ear for being "sassy". It escalated with my age though. Of course it did.

Doesn't it everywhere?

I can't go back to Maldon.

He hooks his thumb under my chin and tilts my face up until I have no choice but to look into his eyes. They're the colour of the centre of a flame, the very palest blue.

A tremor goes through me, and I flush.

I feel safe with Zane, and the combination of safety and him holding me is having an effect I didn't anticipate.

There's something about this man, and I'm struggling to remember why I wanted to get away. Why I should be afraid. Because I'm melting under his white-hot gaze. My mouth opens to get more air in, but it's not from being out of breath after running. Nope. It's pure arousal, unlike anything I've felt. My hips move involuntarily, seeking friction, and his erection presses into my belly.

His eyes narrow, and I freeze.

He was turned on by our chase and our proximity as he holds me... And so am I.

"Why did you take me from the church? Why are you doing this?" I ask the question that has been spinning around my head, and that he avoided while we were in the car. My tone is breathy, revealing my conflict. I shouldn't like being held by Zane, but it feels right in a way that I can't understand, or deny. It's as though all the stars have lined up.

"You don't know?" he replies, an edge to his voice.

My heart sinks in what I'm not ready to call disappointment. Of course. Sex, money, power. One of those reasons.

Money or power doesn't quite make sense. He's gained by taking the Witham territory for himself. Admittedly, no London Mafia Boss has managed to get into the Essex Cartel yet. There is a marriage between a London Mafia Boss and the daughter of Braintree, but that's complicated, so maybe Bethnal thinks if he could marry in too, it might help him?

Well, he'll be disillusioned about that. I have no influence in Maldon.

"You *do* know," he says softly. "I can see it in your face. We're meant to be."

I blink. I must have misheard him.

He strokes his fingers down my throat in a move that

emphasises how I'm at his mercy, but there's no mistaking the hungry expression on his face as his gaze dips to my mouth. "You feel it too. You're mine, little bunny."

Is that what this feeling is? We're fated?

I want to scoff. But I'm an innocent, trapped mafia princess. I haven't a clue about being with a man. I've never responded to anyone like I do to Zane, but I hardly have much to compare to. Maybe this fizzing in my veins is normal?

"How do you know?" I sound confused and not at all as defiant as I intended.

"I'm a forty-two-year-old mafia boss," he states, with a wry hook up of the corner of his mouth that makes my pulse jump.

Oh my. I thought he was older than me, and I was right. He's more than twice my age. That's filthy.

And makes my clit throb.

"I have instincts honed by more than a decade of running the Bethnal mafia." His hand comes to rest over my collarbones, as light and binding as a collar. "Of hard choices, and life-or-death judgements. I trust my gut. And my heart."

It's mad that I understand. My heart says the same— that he's mine and I'm his. Somehow, this feeling is as bone-deep as the lessons of not trusting my family.

He leans in, lowering his mouth until I'm cross-eyed trying to keep looking at him. His breath is warm.

"Say no, little bunny. Say you don't want me to kiss you. Say that you don't feel this too."

He's so close. My lips tingle and my heart races, but I don't say no. I can't.

His thumb strokes over the back of my trapped hand.

"Did you really want to escape me?" The low rumble of

his voice is like the harmony to a song I've been singing all my life, that's out of time with everything in Maldon. I thought I was out of tune. But it's not. I just didn't have the right person with me.

And then he touches his lips to mine.

My first kiss.

4

ZANE

I keep the kiss gentle, holding back my sordid desires. I need to feast on this girl, but instead I give her feathery kisses and slides. I reveal what I want a sliver at a time. Using my breath on her lips and presses and drags, I coax her into passion, drawing out a bit more with every moment that flows by. She responds perfectly, arching into me and parting her soft lips in a little moan.

I continue to trap her wrists, not just to force her to take this sweet kiss, but because holding her captive makes my cock hard in a way that I've never experienced before. A feral part of me I didn't realise existed relishes keeping her trapped and feeding her desires.

And if she's in my hands and out of her mind with lust, she can't run away.

Cupping her jaw, I angle her head to allow me easier access. I slide my tongue into her mouth and swallow her mewl of arousal as I explore and tease. This kiss should feel insubstantial, but it's like the ocean lapping at the shore. It's just a kiss, but my body doesn't appreciate that, and it's stronger than anything I've experienced before. Wetness slides across the helmet of my cock as I shift against my girl. I'm leaking pre-come.

It's sheer chemistry. And it's the same for her, judging by her movements against me. I doubt she is conscious of how she's showing me her arousal. The hitches in her breath, the way she kisses me back, the involuntary shivers.

I drag my lips over her cheek, and down to her neck. She's delicious, sweet and salty on my tongue. I want to explore every part of her. My brain is totally disengaged, and my physical instincts have taken over.

"Fuck, I love you," I mutter hoarsely.

She goes rigid.

Cursing inwardly, I lift my head. Her lips are pink and shiny from our kiss, but there's a pinch between her brows, and she's no longer soft and pliable. Have I scared her? I didn't intend to say that, but it feels right. And sometimes the only way is forward.

"It's true." I'm not taking it back.

"You can't love me," she scoffs, but a tremor in her voice tells a different story. "You've only just met me."

"I can. I do." I look into her dark-green eyes and will her to acknowledge this. "The moment I saw you, I knew. You're my soulmate." I've never believed in that before, but I've never been in love before, either. New experiences all round. "I love you."

I slide my hand up her arm, caressing the delicate skin until I reach where I have her wrists pinned. Then I interlock our fingers and lower our hands. Pressing my body forwards, I keep her in position, captured between my bulk and the solid tree trunk.

She has relaxed, as though she wants to believe.

"Marry me." She was going to wed that prick Witham. This is no different, except that we'll be deliriously happy together, and I'll treat her like a princess. No—she'll be my queen.

She blinks in disbelief. "Why?"

"Because I love you," I repeat patiently.

"You think that now." Shaking her head sceptically, she glances away. "You'll change your mind."

"No, I won't." This feeling is as solid as the ground beneath my feet. "You're it for me. I understand that you don't believe me yet." Though I don't like it. "You need more time."

"*You* need to take a sec to realise you've gone mad." She looks back at me, but despite her words, she's gripping my knuckles with her fingertips, digging her nails in.

"You think I'll stop loving you? Little bunny, love isn't like that. It's not a thing you can turn off. I'll still feel the same in an hour, a week, a month, a year. A decade, a millennium. I'll always love you."

"You've been in love before then, since you know so much about it." Her mouth twists.

Interesting. Is she jealous? My sweet girl. She has nothing to be jealous of.

"Not like you think, no. Not romantically." That calms her a fraction. "But I've witnessed love. I've seen the way it wrecks people."

And until now, I had no idea why anyone would care more for another person than themselves. I thought it was stupid. I didn't realise that once you found the woman who fits and smooths your every jagged edge, that the sensation of coming home would make it impossible to ever turn away.

I could no more let Willow leave me than give up my tattered soul.

"It's a permanent mark. You can't just change your

mind because it's not from your heart. But I've seen people die for those they love, and never understood. Until now, because I'd lay down my life for you, if that was what you needed."

It sounds over the top, but quantum physics is also absurd and true.

"I want you. Whatever you'll allow, I'll have. I'll always crave more, though."

I touch our foreheads together and tighten my grip on her hands, breathing her in. It's a simple thing, but another first. This girl is all of them for me. Every first emotion, all the tender moments I hadn't realised I was missing.

"This is insane," she mutters, almost to herself, but she's holding my hands as much as I am hers. "I'm the sister of your enemy, of an Essex Cartel kingpin. You don't really want this. Let me go. You don't believe what you just said."

Ouch.

I grit my teeth to prevent an outright "No" from emerging, and think. She ran away, but she responded when I kissed her.

She's scared. She's out of control. So far this morning she has been a bride, watched her groom die in front of her, been very publicly kidnapped, thrown herself from a moving car, and been chased down. Without shoes.

I make a mental note to tend to those bare feet later.

Then an obsessed man twice her age announced that he loves her. And I think she feels the same.

I sigh and look into her face.

It's not unreasonable that she would be wary, my flighty little bunny. This is a lot to take in.

Maybe she just needs more time, and the illusion of choice.

"Thing is, you're my payment, Willow."

She sags.

"Ownership is permanent, but I might be persuaded to accept other assets..." I trail off, leaving her to imagine.

"I don't have anything," she says miserably.

I raise one eyebrow.

She huffs. "Literally, I have this blood-splattered dress I'm standing in."

"I'm sorry about the stains, but it wasn't like you were going to wear it again," I point out wryly.

Her lips quirk upwards. "I guess not. Look, I have some money saved," she confesses in a rush. "I'll give it to you. But please, not all of it. I'll need enough to get away."

"Your finances are safe from me. I have more income than you can possibly imagine."

"I could work. I'm a hard worker," she adds, as though she didn't hear me.

"I'm sure you are, but you won't have to while you're with me. I already have a lot of employees. I'm interested in unique delicacies."

A less observant man might not have noticed when her gaze dipped and stuck. She stares at my lips for long seconds before taking in my jaw, where a dark shadow of stubble forms within hours of me shaving. Her pupils dilate, big and black, despite the sunshine through the trees.

"I could give you something else," she says breathlessly, then meets my eyes and pink tinges her cheeks.

"What do you suggest?" It's an enticement.

"I don't know."

"Liar," I respond softly. "You do know."

"I've only got myself."

And such a pretty self. She's everything.

"And I haven't got much experience," she adds in a rush.

"How much?" I demand, my heart hammering once again. Could I claim all of her? Make her mine entirely.

"That was my first kiss," she confesses miserably.

"Oh, little bunny. And I stole it from you." I can't keep the glee from spreading a smile across my face. "What else?"

"I..." She blushes furiously and I shift my feet to better block her from moving. Then I release her hands and wrap my arms around her waist. Her hands flutter to my shoulders.

Stroking the silk over her warm skin with my thumb, I decide I've waited long enough.

"I want one thing from you." *I want everything, but we'll start with this.*

"And then you'll consider that payment, and let me go?"

I swallow razor blades. Can I really agree to that? I'm usually a man who keeps his promises.

"Yes." The blood and pain of that word threaten to choke me, even though I'm certain this will never happen. "If you want to leave after you've fulfilled your debt, I'll..." *Stalk you and protect you for the rest of our lives.* "...Take you somewhere safe myself."

She'd think I've released her, and I'd care for her from a distance, and that amounts to the same thing.

"Okay." She nods, such a proud creature, liking to imagine this is a negotiation. "I'm listening."

"You said you're not experienced. I want *all your firsts*."

Not just her kiss. I want to be the first and *only* man to pleasure and use that perfect body of hers.

She lets out a little whimper.

"Not all at once," I concede. "You can take as much time as you need."

But she should have no illusions. She's mine. And if it

takes us forever to discover all the ways to be together? Well. That's not a problem for me.

Biting her lip, Willow digs her fingers into my shoulders, apparently unaware that her breathing has accelerated.

"And you'll stay with me, as my *guest*, until we're done."

That should be long enough for her to recognise we're meant to be. And for me to find out exactly what she wants, and arrange it. I have to know everything about her. I want to spoil her, and look after her, and for that, we need to spend time together so I can understand her innermost desires.

"All my firsts, but I can say when," she checks.

I nod. "But you stay with me until what you owe is paid, little bunny."

"Okay." She licks her lips nervously, but a spark of excitement flares in her eyes. Then it's my turn to be entranced by her, as she was by me. "No second times, though, right?"

"Agreed." My imagination is extremely vivid. I feel sure we can manage a lifetime of firsts. Unless we want to.

But damn it, I've already had her first kiss.

"Except," I rumble. I shouldn't do this. We only just made the deal.

"Yes?" And her word is more than a question. It's trust, and agreement.

And I'm a mafia boss, not some tame businessman. I need her. Now.

"Fuck it."

5

WILLOW

This time, his kiss is deep and punishing. A forbidden second kiss, my mind acknowledges, but it feels different, a first all its own. Intense and passionate. He's claiming me. My arms slip up of their own accord and slide into his dark hair. It's shockingly soft, and a total contrast to the rough of his stubble.

All my firsts.

It was rash to have agreed, but the moment he said it, I couldn't imagine giving those firsts to anyone but Zane.

I tell myself that I had no choice. That's sane. I had to agree because the tall, dark, handsome mafia boss who stole me away from a wedding I desperately wanted someone to save me from, and held me captive.

That's the only reason.

He told me he loved me in a voice like honey and brandy and sin.

His erection is almost painful digging into my belly. He *wants* me. He picked me up, and chased me. For the first time in my life, to be chosen for myself, like a book from the shelf. Not for money or power, like the man I was supposed to marry this morning.

He runs his palms up by sides, groaning as I kiss him back with as much passion as he's giving me. And in response, I'm fizzing. I'm alive with needs that have been unread pages of my story until now. Between my legs is hot and slick and aching. My nipples are jutting out, and as I press closer to Zane, they're so sensitive.

He parts my knees with his, and I moan as his thigh rubs over my sex.

Oh god, I've never felt like this. I'm ready to explode.

He breaks our kiss, panting, his breath hot on my lips.

"Fuck, I didn't mean to get so..." But then his mouth is on mine again, demanding and passionate, and his hands are roaming over my body. I cling onto him.

Would it be the same with any man? I have all the sexual experience of a tomato, but somehow, I don't think so. This feels special.

"You're writhing against me, Willow." He scrapes my cheek as he shifts to kissing over the line of my jaw, then onto my neck, and my... I... My brain disintegrates when he kisses me there. "What do you want?"

I can't say. I'm just a sugar-high, hormone jelly. I run my hands down his sides, a mewl of desire escaping me as I feel how different from me he is. Muscled, strong, and huge.

More, I want more, but I can't ask. I shouldn't.

"Willow," he says roughly as I reach his waist.

He shifts backwards, and I take advantage, ignoring his warning and then oh... That's his erection. We both gasp as my hand covers the top.

"What are you doing, little bunny?"

Even through the layers of fabric I can feel his heat, and

how hard he is. And *big*. My head is spinning at how enormous his length is.

All my firsts. That will go *inside* me. I'd be stuffed with him, like eating too much and feeling ready to pop, but the sexual version of that.

"Oh no you don't," he snaps, and I realise I've been rubbing my hand over him. Before I can blink, he has grabbed my hands and yanked them back over my head, pinning them again with expert efficiency.

I should apologise or say something sexy, or attempt to use my actual brain, but I don't. I'm on fire with sexual energy I didn't know was in me. Maybe it wasn't. Perhaps it's Zane and the way he's controlling me, firm and dominant, and kinda scary. And yet, gentle too.

"You are not going to seduce me into letting you go." His tone is harsh and icy-blue eyes glare down at me, like a clear day in Antarctica.

I wasn't trying to do that.

Probably I should have been. Would have been smart, but would have required my brain not to be mush.

I pull against his iron grip and inexplicably, that makes me even hotter, and I moan, rubbing myself against him.

His brows lower. "Tell me what you want."

"No." And it's a no to telling him aloud, not to him touching me. I can't say what I want, not least because I'm not sure I know. But I keep trying to get contact between us.

My eyes plead, and I squirm. I'm so achy and incomplete. I *need* to feel him.

His eyebrows lower into a scowl, and he stares at me.

"Do you need me to make you?"

I press my lips together.

Yes. I really want this, but I can't. It's stupid to ask.

"If you want me to stop, just say, 'Zane, stop'." He says

that like the phrase is dirty and hot, and it snakes down my back. "No safe words. No nonsense or codes. Nothing but honesty between us."

He pulls my dress up, and I don't prevent him. I lean onto the tree, pulling my wrists slightly against the grip of his hands and relishing the way he doesn't give in.

"Open your legs," he murmurs, pushing the back of his hand against my inner thigh, and I obey.

His fingers are gentle as he caresses my bare skin, but I tremble. It's fear, right?

God, I'm such a liar.

The words are just there. "Zane, stop."

"You're so young." He sounds tortured. "But I can't not have everything you give and more. I need you. Stop me now..."

I do not want him to stop. I want him to *take*, so I'm not being an idiot, or falling in... Love.

He slides his big hand over my hip with ease, and finds the seam of my knickers.

"Tell me, no, little bunny," he says hoarsely. "We shouldn't be doing this..." But he doesn't hesitate.

I should object as he gently delves beneath the cotton, but instead, I let my head fall back as he reaches where I'm hot and needy. The bark of the tree digs in where I'm levering off it to get closer to him while pretending not to.

"You're wet." There's approval in his words, and satisfaction. He was right.

I close my eyes as I feel a flush creep over my cheeks. I'm a whore. "No."

"You say 'no'." His finger slides effortlessly into my folds. Then he brushes over my clit and I almost levitate, my body electrified. "But this says 'yes', little bunny."

But I writhe, trying to get his fingers where I need them.

He chuckles softly, and circles my clit with an expert touch, making me shake and pant. His pressure is perfect. Not too hard or too soft like I did when I first discovered how to pleasure myself. Zane's confidence and competence is a turn-on like I've never imagined.

I've been told stories about the London Mafia Bosses since I can remember words. They're said to be brutal, uncompromising, power hungry, and arrogant. Bethnal Green is supposed to be one of the worst.

And I can't deny that there's truth in what was said. Zane is all those things. But he's also intoxicating. His attention focused on me makes me glow.

A cocky London Mafia Boss.

But is it really ego when he's this amazing? Because he is that good.

I'm so close, wriggling to get more. To have that extra that will tip me off the edge.

"Such a needy girl, soaked for me," His voice is low and rough. "You want this as much as I do, don't you?"

I moan as he moves his hand down, and with no warning, his fingertip finds my entrance. Seamlessly, the flat of his thumb rubs my clit, and it's even better. Then he pushes.

"Open," he commands.

There's a pinch that makes me gasp, then he drives his finger deeper and it feels amazing.

"That's it. You're being such a good girl for me." He slips in and out as he runs over my clit in firm lines, and the feeling of being stroked from inside and out is intoxicating. "Let me in."

Seamlessly, he slides another finger in, and I choke out a cry.

"Good girl," he soothes me again, his voice honey and

brandy dripping off a spoon. "You like that? My cock will be even better."

The flex of his hips presses the heated iron bar of his erection against my stomach and the touch of discomfort only heightens my pleasure. That and the frisson of fear. He's big, and I'm tiny by comparison. How would it feel...?

I imagine him ripping open his trousers and shoving into me right here, and yes, my god, I want that. To have him overwhelm me.

"Come all over my fingers, little bunny," he croons. "Give me all your cream. I'll take care of you. I'll make it so pleasurable. I'll give you babies too. You'd like that, wouldn't you?"

I can't say yes, but I'm nodding against his chest. Or am I writhing with need because I'm so close to orgasm? The way he's holding me pinches in a dozen different places, but he's careful. I can tell, even through the fog of ecstasy that has enveloped my mind, that he's aware of every part of me.

"Zane..."

He's still before I've finished the word.

My eyes fly open and he's looking down at me. He hasn't let go, but he's stopped. There's a taut silence as he slowly withdraws his fingers.

"No, no." I'm confused and tug against his hand that's still holding mine. "Please."

"Willow," he breathes seriously, his eyes shards of ice. "What are you saying?"

"Please, give me..." I'm so worked up, I'm practically incoherent. "Please, make me..."

He waits.

"Make me come," I sob out the confession.

"My love. I'll give you everything." Then his fingers

slide back into my slit, and he's moving harder. "Good girl for asking. All you ever have to do is ask."

Then his fingers shove into my passage, beckoning me, and I shatter into a million pieces, the pleasure spiked and quick even as it repeats, pulsing through me with his clever caresses.

The bliss is so intense that my legs give way, and I slump, but he holds me secure. I'm buzzing and all my focus is on the places where he and I touch.

A chirping bird intrudes.

Then the cool of the tree trunk and the dig of pain into my back, and the sunshine on my cheek.

The rise and fall of his chest and the loosening of his grip on my hands until he guides them to flop against his chest.

The shame comes last, and it's weak, unable to overcome the satisfaction of being the centre of this big, powerful man's world. For now, at least.

I make a vague sound of dissent as he bends, but this time when he scoops me up, I'm cradled in his arms, not over his shoulder. The essence of Zane mixes with the clean outdoorsy-ness of the forest, and I give in again, breathing it in. Sandalwood and musk.

The men of the Maldon mafia never smelled this good. All I know is, it's good. He has a compulsive scent that makes me want to bury my nose into his skin and rub my face over him. It's like he has new-book smell.

Forcing myself away from his book-like pheromones, or whatever it is I'm responding to, I look around.

"This isn't the way we came." I didn't take much notice, but the woodland is different here, and there's more undergrowth. Fewer crunchy copper-coloured leaves.

"Nope," he agrees. "It's a shortcut."

"Where to?"

But there's no reason for him to answer, because at that moment we emerge from the forest at the bottom of a grass avenue lined with trees. It leads to an imposing red brick mansion with ivy growing up the walls and lilac flowers over the porch. Zane Bethnal's country residence.

I'm in a white silk wedding dress, being carried by a strong, handsome man who says he loves me, towards the sort of place dreams are made of.

I should pinch myself. Does that even work? I've not tried it in a dream, and actually, upon reflection, I don't want to wake up. This is the best dream I've had for a long time.

So I remain silent as Zane carries me to the house. He nods slightly as he points out the tennis courts off to the side, that there are stables, and a rose garden.

It's a mansion. That was obvious from a distance, but the second Zane steps inside, the door opened by one of his men, it's breathtaking. The wallpaper is a painting of leaves, flowers, and birds, the floor is an intricate geometric pattern made from gleaming wood, and the whole entrance hall is flooded with light from a glass dome above.

"Aren't you going to put me down?" I ask halfway up the double, curved wooden staircase.

"So you can run and hurt your feet again?" he responds dryly, turning at the top and entering the first door, skilfully opening it without even shifting my weight in his arms. "No."

"Just gonna carry me around like I'm your lapdog? I want a diamante collar and steak every day."

His chest vibrates as he laughs, and I'm stupidly happy

that he likes my jokes. None of my family ever did. Do. Am I talking about them as though they're gone already?

Maybe it's true that they're in my past, since I have just been kidnapped by their enemy.

All my firsts.

He kicks the door closed behind him, and I examine the room from my place tight in his arms. It's painted a deep green-blue with accents of pale grey. The furniture is all free-standing dark wood. No space-saving fitted wardrobes here, nope.

"Don't move," he instructs severely as he places me onto the enormous four-poster bed. The sheets have an expensive sheen, and I secretly caress them as I watch him.

He strides across the room, through another door to what seems to be a bathroom decked with those small rectangular white tiles. He busies himself in a cupboard, his back to me.

I split my attention between my captor and looking around. The windows are that old-fashioned type with two sets of six panes of glass, and look out over the huge lawn that leads down to a lake, and the endless blue and cloud-patterned sky. I'm used to comfort since my family is wealthy enough. But it's all new money, all shiny steel, magnolia paint, and glass. None of the refinement that Bethnal's house has.

"Is this your bedroom?" I can't see much to indicate that. It's austere. Everything in its place, behind doors, except for a watch on the bedside cabinet.

"It's yours now, too." He returns and I look up at him. Up, and up, because he towers over me, intimidating and thrilling. Mine too?

But I don't have time to examine that thought, because

he scoops me into his arms, and I let out a squeak and instinctively cling to him. In response he merely holds me tighter, as though he understands my need to be secure.

The bathroom has two big marble sinks, a shower that you could do laps of, and an enormous roll top bath. Only one toothbrush, I note.

"Do you have a wife, or a girlfriend?" I ask as he sits me on the edge of the bath. It's partly filled, and I whine as my feet touch the warm water, the dress rucked over my thighs. The water releases all the pain I've been ignoring.

"It wouldn't hurt if you hadn't run from me," he chastises me in an undertone.

My feet sting, and I gaze at where brown and red float off my toes. Mud and blood from where I ran from Zane. He's right, but I don't regret making him chase me down.

"And no, I don't have a wife or girlfriend." He's moved around to the other side of the bath, and leans on the edge, regarding me levelly. "There hasn't been anyone for years. But now there's you."

He reaches down and it takes me a second to realise what he's doing. He's rolled up his sleeves, revealing a pattern of black tattoos over his forearms, and picks up a pristine white washcloth. His arms are bulky and strong, and as he lifts my foot. I'm too shocked to object, and too entranced by the muscles in his shoulders and upper arms as he cleans my foot. The tattoos—mainly patterns, but I can identify eyes disfigured in various ways, and some kind of long blackberry fruits held in a skeleton hand, the red juice dripping over the bone—disappear up under his shirt.

I want to see what he looks like when he's fully revealed. It's a sensation I've never had before. Boys haven't interested me, but Zane...

He has a gentle touch, and he makes low, rumbling

sounds of apology but says nothing when I wince and hiss as he picks out the grit and mud and brushes the small cuts until both my feet are perfectly pink. A London mafia boss cleans my tootsies without a word, as though this is completely normal.

6

ZANE

Willow's feet are small and delicate in my big hands, and this whole thing is arousing in ways I cannot explain, even though the little cuts make me want to roar with fury at whoever did this to her. Which is unfortunate, since it's her and me.

I like caring for Willow, which is new. I've been more likely to kill than comfort for a long time.

When I'm convinced that her feet are perfectly clean and anything more would be obvious that I just need to touch her, I lift her legs and steady her shoulder so she's out of the bath without having been caught up in that impractical dress.

My fingers stay on her upper arms for a second longer than strictly necessary.

I force myself to let go.

"There's a shower if you prefer." My hands twitch towards her, and I take a distinct step backwards to prevent myself. Not touching her feels wrong, so wrong. But it can't be helped. "Or run the bath again."

One more movement away and it's torture. But while I

will steal a kiss, give her what she needs, and accept no fucking nonsense about looking after her, even I know that we aren't at the "share a shower" point. Yet.

"I'll leave you to it."

I'm at the door when her small voice says the word I want to hear on her lips constantly.

"Zane."

7

WILLOW

He stops instantly and turns, and my heart bounces. Is it that easy for me to have his attention if I want it? The words stick in my throat on a lump that has formed.

His expression is steady and serious as he waits with apparently endless patience.

"I can't get out of this on my own," I confess.

Only his eyes move, scanning down the wedding dress.

"It has ties at the back. No zip. And I can't undo them."

He stalks around me—that sounds silly, but it really is the only word for it—and I stand perfectly still, as though I'm his little prey again. Like if I don't move, and don't attract attention, I'll escape.

The first touch of his hands to my silk-covered back is so gentle I shouldn't even be able to feel it. But I'm attuned to this man in some way I can't explain.

He sighs deeply.

"What is it?"

"The knots tightened when you ran from me." There's a hint of judgement in his tone, and he pauses. "Do you like this dress?"

"No. I *hate* it." I didn't know I felt quite so strongly until someone—Zane—asked me my opinion.

"Good."

He's across the room and back before I can ask what he's doing.

"Don't move."

I freeze.

The corset pulls tight at my waist, then there's a crackle of metal into fabric, and it releases.

"Good girl."

A blade slides up my spine and I'm breathless. He shifts the scissors, and the point presses into my skin. A shiver goes through me.

"Totally still," he says sharply. "I don't want to hurt you."

Each snip of the scissors slices through the air. Then it's off, and I'm free and pulling in breath like it had been choking me, which is ridiculous, because I ran in this stupid dress. But the relief is like it was chains not ribbon holding me into it.

"So beautiful." A single warm finger brushes down my spine. "You're mine, Willow. Sooner or later, you'll discover that." Zane's kiss at my nape is unexpected, but soft and chaste and possessive in a way I can't even begin to describe.

Then he's out of the bathroom, leaving me alone.

As I finish undressing, I'm not sure what I wish had happened. I hesitate before stepping beneath the huge shower head, the feeling of Zane shimmering on my skin again. Then I force myself in, and the warm water soaks me from head to foot. Or at least, I tell myself it's the shower and the deliciously scented toiletries I find. Every single one is in a thick bottle that states wealth. They smell like Zane, and I close my eyes and breathe it in. The water washes away the sweat and the tension and it's impossible to feel worry about the future with the clouds of steam around me.

Zane is on the other side of the door, and I haven't locked it. He could walk in, and I couldn't stop him. He could get into the shower, naked, trap me between the cool tiles and his massive, hot body, and reach between my legs again.

I'm washing my thighs, and my fingers have found their way to where I'm wet and *slick*, not just with water. And sensitive. I'm on edge and tingly.

My shower thoughts have taken an inappropriate direction.

Touching myself in his shower... I shouldn't.

However much I let the water flow there, I can't stop the image of Zane and how I felt as he held and fingered me against the tree, or even the sweetness of being carried and having my feet washed. It's as though all my nerve endings have lit up with his proximity.

My clit throbs.

And so do my feet.

Gulping, I move my hand away and dive out of the shower. The towel from the rack is so fluffy and white that it could have been stolen from the sky. It almost drags on the floor when I wrap it around my chest.

It's only when I see the wedding dress flopped and ruined on the tiled floor like the crumpled tissue of a giant with a nosebleed, that I realise I have another problem.

Clutching the towel, I creep the door open.

"Little bunny." His voice is a purr from the other side of the room. He's rubbing his hair with a towel, and it's messy in a way that makes him look much younger, even as the silver in it glistens. Dressed in jeans and a black-blue T-shirt, he takes me in at a glance.

"Sit." He points at his bed.

"Woof," I mutter, but I obey meekly. There is a first-aid kit on the dark, smooth covers.

His eyes are light with amusement as he kneels before me so we're the same height. He really is absurdly tall.

I have no idea what he's going to do, and then he takes my foot in his hand.

"You don't need to..." I begin, only to be silenced by his hard look.

"You're mine to care for."

With steady hands, he applies antiseptic and little flexible clear dressings, pausing when I hiss from the sting. He does it all with absolute care and attention, as though he really did love me.

Scary thought. But not as strange as it was when he first said it.

"Thank you," I say when he sits back, still loosely holding one of my ankles in his big hand, like he's reluctant to let me go. Or perhaps it's a cuff to prevent me from running again.

He nods, his brows low.

"I was going to ask about what to wear. Should I put the wedding dress—"

"No," he cuts me off. "And as much as I like you in that towel, you'll be more comfortable in clothes that won't fall off with a..." He brushes the back of his free hand against the towel, and I cling to it.

He smiles and tilts his head in an "I was right" indication. "Do you want me to pick you something out from my wardrobe, or choose for yourself?"

"I'll decide," I say impulsively, then bite my lip. Apparently not choosing my own wedding dress has left a bigger mark than I thought.

"Work clothes are in there." He points at the massive wardrobe that's straight out of a kid's movie. His fingers still lightly hold my ankle, and it's as though he's totally forgotten to let go. "Casual clothes in the chest of drawers."

I blink. "Are you suggesting I pick through your stuff?"

"You won't find anything that will hurt you. Or me." He smiles wryly, and I have to stop myself from throwing myself into his arms. "Go ahead. I have a couple of things I need to sort."

He sinks into an armchair by the window that looks out over the garden where we walked up from the wood, takes out his phone, and begins to tap and swipe as though he's checking emails.

You can tell a lot about someone by looking at their possessions, I think. I study the contents of his wardrobe. It's all simple, of the finest quality. There are lots of suits that are in fabric so tightly woven that I can hardly make out the lines, in red-back or dark grey. The shirts are more varied, with white in different weights of fabric, every shade of a red the colour of wine, or blue-green. Then more in greys that range from a thin stripe on white to almost black.

Zane said he had something he needed to do, but despite that, and the lure of the gorgeous view, whenever I peek at him from the corner of my eye, he's watching me.

That heats me all over.

I move to his large chest of drawers, and while they look heavy, the drawer slides out easily. The ease of quality that's made to last. I blush when I find that it's his underwear. Of course it is. It's the top drawer, silly. But though I'm redder than a strawberry, I don't close it quickly like I should. I take in the carefully separated piles of smooth, black boxer briefs, plain dark socks in neat pairs, and the cufflinks and watches that are so understated they can only be expensive.

The next drawer has T-shirts, again tidy, and in the same colour palate as his suits. Then stacks of jeans, and some casual shorts. Everything is in its place.

I'm building up a picture of a man who is almost pathologically controlled, but has an affinity for black and deep blues and greens and the red that's like the berries I saw in his tattoos. I don't dare ask him about any of that. He's calm and confident, but observant as I examine every garment he wears. Touching the cloth that sits next to his skin feels safe by comparison to looking at him, and feeds what is rapidly becoming a compulsion.

I choose a T-shirt that's almost as large as my bedsheet at home and the grey sweatpant shorts, and take both to the bathroom to put on. I leave my knickers folded up within the dress, and observe myself in the floor-to-ceiling mirror.

I'd look sexier with just the T-shirt, or a crisp white shirt. I know this. But I chose the safer option. I don't have a bra because the corset on the dress didn't allow one, and my nipples are sensitive against the T-shirt.

"So, what now?" I ask as I emerge back into the room where Zane is waiting.

He looks me up and down lazily, from my still damp hair to my bare feet. He's not even pretending that he isn't mentally stripping off these clothes.

All my firsts.

Is that going to include taking my heart?

8

ZANE

I regard Willow in my gym clothes. I like the way my shorts seem oversized, rucked at the waist where she's tied the strings, and my T-shirt is so big on her I can only see a few inches of those shorts anyway.

"Suits you."

She rolls her eyes. "I look like a puppy got into a laundry basket."

"You do look cute, I'll give you that. But not like a puppy."

"I think that's an insult," she replies, mock offended. "Puppies are great."

"Yes, but I don't get hard-ons for puppies."

"Not even this type?" She flattens the T-shirt over her breasts, revealing that her nipples are pebbled.

Fuck, this girl. She's going to match me at every turn. "I like that type, yeah. Though I'm distracted by your legs at the moment."

She shakes her head and gives a huff of sceptical laughter as I lead her into the kitchen.

I pull out a chair at the table, and wait while she peeks

from under her eyelashes, taking in the black-grey cabinets with brass fittings. The darkness makes her look angelic by comparison.

She sits, and although I intend to push in her chair like a gentleman—making the attempt, anyway—she pulls up one knee protectively.

"Are you hungry? I am." Mainly for her rather than food.

"Kidnap is hard work, huh?" She watches me with cautious eyes.

"I asked because orgasms can give you the munchies."

"So does trying to escape."

"What would you like?" I ask. Let's move the conversation away from why she's here, and onto why she'll love being here.

"What are my choices?"

"Anything. You can have anything you want." I'd present this girl with her enemy's head on a plate without a blink.

She narrows her eyes, as she thinks. "We could go to a restaurant?"

"You want a formal dinner? We'll go to Bethnal and there's any cuisine you fancy." I open the fridge to hide my smile, and I'm pleased to find it well stocked. "But don't you need a snack beforehand, to keep your energy up for your next escape attempt?"

I glance over my shoulder and yes, that was definitely a twitch of her lips upwards. "Wow," she deadpans. "Might be almost a date, rather than a kidnap."

"First date?" I ask, though I think I know the answer, and I'm waiting like it's Christmas.

"Yes." Her voice is softer for that acknowledgement. "Are you going to cook?"

"Yeah." I lean my hip against the black marble counter. "I had a decent kitchen installed when I bought this house. I'll make you something you'll like."

She hesitates, then nods, and fuck that glimmer of trust lights me up. I busy myself by selecting what I need from the cupboards, then chop the juicy fresh tomatoes I found and set them neatly aside.

"You clear up as you go," she says as I give the chopping board a quick rinse, then dry it and cut the bread.

"Yeah, force of habit. I didn't always have staff to do everything."

She watches curiously, as though I'm very odd to her. "What are you making?"

"Poor man's pizza."

"What?" She laughs with disbelief.

"Bread, chopped tomatoes, grated cheese." I point at the ingredients in turn. I'll sprinkle some herbs on too. "It's like pizza, but very low budget."

Wriggling to get more comfortable on the chair, she examines me as though I'm a puzzle she'd like to solve. "I thought you said you were rich."

"Mmm," I agree, and continue putting it all together, slathering the whole thing in cheese. "I am very wealthy, but I wasn't when I was a kid."

"So poor you couldn't afford pizza?"

I nod and stand back once the food is under the grill. "Yeah. And I still make my own snacks sometimes."

She doesn't take her eyes off me as I put out plates and toast the cheese to perfection—no walking away or getting distracted when I'm making food for Willow. I have this urge I've never felt for a woman before. I want to care for Willow, and impress her. I want her to approve of everything I am, and decide to stay.

Bit of a problem, since I'm a grumpy homicidal mafia boss. But for her, maybe I could be something else... Just for *her*.

Our plates aren't fancy when I place them on the table. Salad on the side, and what amounts to cheese on toast. I sit opposite her and dig in, picking it up with my fingers, and she copies me.

"This is very informal. I didn't think that was a London mafia boss' style." She takes the first bite as though the food might hurt her, then her eyes go wide as she chews.

"Good?"

She wordlessly takes another mouthful, then another, and I think that's a yes. We stuff our faces with carbohydrates and fat and that tangy acidicness that makes the whole thing irresistible.

"Not what you get in Maldon?" I ask lightly.

"Huh, none of my family would lower themselves to eat something called *poor*. Never mind cook for themselves."

"Missing out." I finish eating only just before Willow.

"You wolfed that down, little bunny," I tease. "I told you. Hungry work."

She blushes prettily and for a second, I think she's going to acknowledge the chemistry that fizzes between us.

"Boss," a voice interrupts from behind me.

Fuck.

Willow looks across at Agombar, the manager of my affairs when I'm in Suffolk.

"Miss, your clothes have arrived."

"My clothes?" She turns to me.

I'm not ready to give up this time with her and me relaxing, with my girl in my T-shirt, but like an idiot, the consequences of my own decisions are here.

So I rise and hold out my hand to her, and although I

half expect her to ignore it, she slips her little fingers over mine, and doesn't let go as I lead her through the house. I'm not sure what I'll see when I throw open the doors to the ballroom, but Willow's gasp is gratifying.

"What is this?" Her eyes flash white as she stares around the room, that's full of racks of clothes.

"You needed something to wear," I say. "A local boutique was happy to help."

"Happy?" she echoes sceptically.

"Well paid."

She shakes her head, but approaches the nearest rail, and picks up a top. "You did all this for me?"

"It's only one shop, sorry." We need to re-adjust her sense of what's due to her. "We'll try another tomorrow. You can tell me which, in fact. Or just order online with my credit card, but I know you needed clothes. Cute as you are in mine, they don't fit that well."

"What?" she splutters, looking up from where she's trailing her hands over a rack of tops. "You'll make another shop put its whole stock into your... What even is this room?"

"It's a ballroom, and yes."

"That's silly."

"It's really not." She deserves everything, but I can't let her out of my sight just yet. We'll get to that, but right now my need to see her, to possess her, is too raw. "I don't hold many balls. None in fact. Perhaps this could be your permanent boutique?" I'm teasing, but I'm also not teasing. Would that make her happy?

She snorts and picks up a pair of blue-green heels and looks at them with a longing expression. "Even more ridiculous than giving me your credit card. I could spend a lot of money, you know?"

"I hope you will." And I mean that. I'd like it if she finds all the ways my money and power can make delight and spoil her.

"A new wedding dress, Zane? Really?" She drifts to the rack of dresses and pulls out one that's long white silk.

"Nice choice." *She could marry me in that.* "I'll change into a suit, and you can wear it to dinner, runaway bride."

"I didn't run, I was carried," she mutters, but there's a spark in her eyes as she glances across at me. "Kidnapped."

9

WILLOW

There are butterflies in my tummy as Zane leans over and does my belt for me in the helicopter. I'm wearing the long, slinky white silk dress that I pulled from the rack earlier with a pair of utterly impractical but gorgeous blue-green shoes with an ankle strap. I almost chose flats, but Zane promised to carry me, and despite having changed into a formal suit again, did just that, striding across the grass to the helicopter carrying me chest to chest, his arms beneath my bottom.

As the sun is lowering in the sky, yellow-gold we land on the top of Zane's London tower block headquarters, which are as stern and simple as his country house is grand. We ride down in the elevator, and he tells me my options for where to eat, detailing who owns each restaurant, how long they've been there, and how good they are at paying their protection fee.

"Protection from what?" I ask as we walk into the lobby. It's modest, but there are armed guards who nod deferentially to Zane as he passes. They're not men in suits, they're in black T-shirts and dark jeans, and have tattoos like the ones under Zane's suit, and they look at him as though he's one of them, but more than.

"Essex," Zane says baldly. His hand hovers at the small of my back when he ushers me out onto the street, where a limo is waiting. "And this is London. There are a few unsavoury characters."

"Oh." I blink up at him. I'm not dressed for running away. Again. You'd think I'd learned my lesson, but despite this silk dress, I feel so dainty next to Zane, and I can't take seriously the idea of any threat that could get through him. "Is it dangerous?"

I glance around us. The serious grey tower block is surrounded by old red-brick houses and trees line the street. There are kids playing down by a park, and under a railway bridge is a bright mural of a tree with black and red berries.

"No." He pauses at the limo and looks down at me. "You know the saying that there used to be a Bobby on every corner, so if you were lost, ask one for directions?"

"Uh, no?" I hide my embarrassment with a little laugh. "You got another first from me. I have literally never heard that."

"You really are young." He winces. "A policeman. Police were in the street, as a public service almost."

The limo door is being held open for us as we stand in the warm evening street.

"And now?"

He shrugs. "Now it's Bethnal men. And we don't allow any woman to be harassed."

I think of his rage in the church. It all seems genuine.

"So what do you want to eat?" he says lightly.

"Um. The first one." I choose at random. It's like my decision-making skills aren't fully developed since my family didn't give me choices. Or maybe just that I think that any of what Zane offers I would like.

"Good choice. Sita's, please Levy," he says to the driver and slides in beside me.

The restaurant turns out to be the sort of place where you're met at the door with a drink, and they welcome Zane with what seems like genuine enthusiasm that's baffling to me because there's respect behind it, not fear. Bethnal isn't like Maldon. Not at all.

The whole dinner date is a warm hug. We're both dressed too fancy—Zane in his suit and me in the white silk dress—but it doesn't matter, because there's so much to say. The menu is all things that make my mouth water, and when I can't decide, Zane just sends the waiter away time after time, never hurrying me, then eventually suggests he just order one of everything for himself and I can share, which forces me to make a choice. Because that's excessive.

I have a couple of regrets though, since the food is as amazing as Zane promised. Delicate and fresh, but with chewy bread on the side.

It's a small table, and the restaurant is intimate, with lighting just over each table that makes the burble of voices and low music around us fade away. Is it an excuse when he passes me the butter and his thumb strokes down my palm?

We sit and talk, him asking again about my imaginary bookshop. What's weird is how much he wants to know about me. His eyes flare ice-cold whenever I let slip about how things are with my family. He looks like a snowstorm when I mention the time my brothers stole all my books and burned them.

Boys will be boys, my mother said at the time.

I try to change the topic, and he tells me about Bethnal's history, from boxing to the markets and parks. It's not enough though, and leaves me desperate to know more about him, not just the territory he's rightly proud of.

When I steal a French fry from his plate, he rolls his eyes and nudges the rest over to me, and there's a flirtatious edge when he dips his finger into my dessert and licks it clean.

I blush. I totally blush.

He talks easily about his territory, but doesn't offer much about himself, and I dare not ask, though curiosity builds in me.

This man. I like him too much. He's gruff and hard, but charming.

"How was your first date?" he asks as we leave, walking out into the velvet night glowing with orange lights.

"Really good," I admit, and our eyes meet.

"They'll all be good. All your firsts."

And suddenly, I can't breathe, despite us being out in the cool, fresh air. He hasn't kissed me all evening, and although his protective hand is at my back, I need more.

"Where shall we go?" he asks casually. "There are bars."

"Can we go home?" I blurt out.

He tilts his head. "You want…"

I need to touch him. There's an energy shimmering between us that has to have an outlet soon or I might burst.

"To the house," I say. I don't even know what it's called, and I don't want to explain to him or to myself why that place feels like it's *ours*. Bethnal is gorgeous, but it's his London territory. Here he's a kingpin, through and through.

There, I think he's Zane. And he's *mine*.

He tips my chin up with his forefinger and strokes his thumb across my lips. "Home."

10

ZANE

I'm not ready for this evening to end. I never will be. So once we're *home*—fuck I like the sound of that—I suggest we have a drink. I take her into the lounge, which is a dark, luxurious room with touches of gold. It's not really my thing, but it's impressive and if Willow thinks this house is home, then it's home for me. We sit with glasses of whiskey that neither of us drinks, and continue talking.

The special editions she'd stock, the paperbacks. The way she'd lay out the shelves and the books she'd choose—apparently photos of people on covers are utterly cringe. I had no idea. She's midway through telling me about the fantasy series that she'd have hardback copies of, and how the romance will have a special section all its own, when she stops, almost mid-sentence.

She gets up and comes over to me, her expression unsure.

I swirl the whiskey in my glass and look up at her. "What are you doing, little bunny?"

"I was thinking," she says, not quite bridging the gap between us. She looks reluctant and I nearly stop her, but instead wait as she decides, trying not to let it show how much I want her close. "I'm scared, but..."

"There's nothing to be scared of when we're together. I'll protect you against everything." This change of topic is confusing.

"Everything except you. I want..." She tails off, still so sweet and vulnerable and innocent and unsure.

"Tell me," I command, drawing the word slowly.

"Something like what you did for me in the woods, but I'd do it for you."

That steals my breath. Another hot, intense kiss? Her fingers around my cock? Her big eyes watching my face and her body pressed to mine, her hand between us as she makes me come.

Fuuuuccckkk so hot, even in my imagination.

"Are you going to chase me, little bunny?" I tease instead of pushing, but make space for her to stand between my feet. "Because the wolf can run away from the bunny, but that's not usually how the game is played."

That makes her smile, and my heart flip-flops. She's cute and sexy. Her dark hair tumbles over her shoulders and that slinky white dress. My god, I can't believe she was getting married only a few hours ago. The idea of anyone else touching her is enough to make jealous rage boil under my skin.

She runs her hand down my chest, over my shirt and as she leans in, I hold my breath. Is she going to initiate a first?

But do I not get a kiss? That's my thought as she slides to her knees before me. Yeah, this beautiful girl on her knees and reaching for my belt, and I wish I had her on my lap and her lips on mine.

But then, we agreed firsts but no repeats, and perhaps she thinks that means she doesn't have to kiss me again.

Fuck. I'd give anything for her to *want* to kiss me.

And in the time that it takes for her hands to get to my waist, my cock has fully hardened, stretching the fabric covering it, and showing as a long outline.

"That's it," I encourage her as she fumbles with my belt, then groan as the underside of her hand brushes the sensitive tip. I'm already on edge, even before the zip sounds a loud rasp and there's the rustle of her tugging just enough for my cock to spring up from my boxer briefs. She blinks, looking at my erection.

"It's..." Her dark-green eyes are bright as she glances up at me. "Beautiful."

"It's all yours," I tell her gruffly.

She leans forward and cautiously covers the head with her mouth. I groan, because fuck, there is nothing as arousing as watching this girl. My cock twitches, and she gasps as it touches her lip.

She looks up at me. "It's hotter than I expected."

"You thought I'd be cold?" I quirk an eyebrow at her. Her curiosity is a delight, even as my balls tighten with the need to have her *now*.

"They call it a trouser snake," she shoots back, and I grin.

"Does that make you a snake charmer?"

Her brows pucker and for a moment I'm sure she's going to confess that this is the first time she's done this. "Will you show me how to make it good for you?"

It is her first then. Warmth spreads in my chest. "If that's what you want. But it will be everything I want however you do it."

"Even like this?" she teases, brushing her bared teeth over where I'm most sensitive and I grab her hair to stop her going further.

"I'd take it from you." Any pain, any pleasure. "But I bet you'll make me come harder if you cover your teeth and suck me."

She seems to consider this, lightly kissing the tip where a bead of pre-come has formed, and licking her lips, looking up at me from beneath her long fan of eyelashes and a groan tears from my throat.

Then she does as I said, stretching her lips and pushing the crown of my cock into her mouth.

We let out dual moans as I hit the limit.

"Fuck that feels so good, Willow." I urge her head to a better angle. "Now take me deeper."

Those pretty green eyes watch me as she adjusts, and obeys.

"Like that. Perfect." And yeah, the pleasure is enough to make my blood pressure cardiac arrest-worthy, but I don't really mean that. I mean the way she gazes at me as though I'm the one who is giving her a gift.

"You look so hot with your lips around my cock. You're taking it like such a good girl." I stroke my hand down her hair as she eases into a rhythm, and when she purrs it sends pleasure vibrating through me, I do it again. "I love—" I catch myself before I repeat my feelings. Once is enough for now. "Your hair. It's beautiful."

I caress her head, encouraging her with a brief tightening in the silk of her hair, and fuck, the feeling of her hot wet mouth on me is ecstasy.

"You can use your hand on the part that you can't fit— oh fuck." She immediately takes that as a challenge as well as an instruction and pushes my cock further into her throat, and I nearly explode that second. Then her hand pumps at my base, gathering the mixture of pre-come and spit that has pooled there and my muscles turn into cooked noodles. Except for my hands, which are now both fisted in her hair, encouraging her.

She's obviously never done this before. She's sloppy, and uncertain, but I'm responding as though I'm as inexperienced as she is. I can't help the shudders as she grips my thigh and begins to suck me fully.

She's going to torture me. There was me thinking I'd die in a mafia shootout, but no. I'll be killed by how it feels to have her mouth on me.

"You're so good at this," I tell her, my voice gravelly.

She hums in approval at my praise. She likes that, huh?

"You look amazing. The way your mouth is stretched on my cock? Willow, you have perfect lips."

I'm helpless for her. Even as I guide her with my hand in her hair, encouraging her faster, it's me who is in her power. If she asked, I'd beg. I'd get onto my knees and plead with her to stay. To let me inside her tight, sweet pussy and let me breed her. Ask her to be my wife.

And yeah, to suck me until I spill in her mouth.

Tingles go up and down my spine.

"You're going to destroy me, little bunny. Do you want me to come in your mouth? Give you the whole big load to taste? To swallow it all and fill your belly?"

Her response is to speed up and a groan tears from my chest.

My hips are lifting in time with her every movement now, fucking up into her mouth as I pull her head down. It's too much for an innocent girl, but I can't not. She unleashes something wild in me.

She shifts slightly, and I see her thighs press together.

"Do you like my dick in your mouth?" I ask, and she whines in response. "Is it making you wet?"

Another noise that I know means "yes", and I shove her

hand off my thigh. "Touch yourself," I order abruptly. "Make yourself come."

She hesitates.

"Now," I snap. I can't take this much longer, and I have to have her with me.

Her loss of focus and pace as she scrabbles to lift her dress is a good thing, because it gives me some respite. Something to think about that isn't how her hot, wet mouth is heaven like I've never experienced before. Then her fingers slip into her knickers and her gaze lifts to my face again, and I'm absolutely lost.

"Is your little pink cunt all wet for me?" I growl. "I bet your clit is swollen and needy."

She whines in agreement and her hand on my cock slows as she loses concentration. That allows me to regather my thoughts, and really see her again. My pretty girl begins to shake as she rubs herself.

"I can't wait to spread your legs and eat you like my personal feast and have you come all over my face. I'm going to savour everything I take from you." My voice is husky with need, and I stare at her, enjoying this moment, even if I can't see her pussy as I'd like. "You'll beg for it. You'll get on your knees, as you are now, and plead with me to do it all again, because you'll be so addicted to the feel of my cock inside you."

It's her throat on my cock that first reveals that she's coming. She stills, unable to do anything but ride her orgasm, and moan.

"Good girl," I tell her, and it defies logic, but just knowing she's found her pleasure pushes me over, despite the lack of stimulation. My balls pull up and seed jets into her mouth. It's a full-body experience, and I tighten my grip on her hair as much to hold onto the spinning world as to keep her on me.

"It's yours, little bunny." I spurt more and more, filling her mouth. "Take it all."

It's white-hot sparks.

And it's intense for her too. She's shuddering and wrecked, her eyes closed, holding my cock like it's her anchor in a storm. She pants and a bit of come drips from the corner of her lips.

"Swallow," I growl.

Her throat bobs as she lifts her head and gazes into my eyes. The savage satisfaction that she's drinking my come is a bolt through me as good as the pulses of the orgasm. Then she licks her lips, and I swear her smile could light the whole of London. She looks proud of herself, and she has every right to be.

"Good girl, good girl." I grab her under the armpits and pull her up onto my lap.

And I nearly kiss her, ducking my head, then stopping at the last second.

I want to. I stare at her mouth for the space of two breaths before I press her to me instead, wrapping my arms around her.

She turns her head so our cheeks touch, hers so soft against mine.

"You did so well," I whisper into her ear and stroke her hair. "You're incredible. A perfect first time."

I expect the praise to bring her closer, but at the word first—a reminder of our bargain—she breathes in as though bracing herself, and sits back. Then, avoiding looking into my face, she climbs off my lap.

"Steady," I say as she wobbles and her mouth sets in a mulish line.

She shakes out the skirt of her long dress and regards me, from beneath her lashes like a wary forest creature reminded of its cage. "Will you release me once we have sex?"

No.

"You seem to be forgetting some firsts you've promised me," I drawl. I'm going to be an uncompromising bastard about this, but I don't give a fuck. She's never leaving. "Have you screamed my name as I ate your pussy?"

That widens her eyes. She didn't realise I meant that sort of first, too.

"No."

"What about your arse?" I lounge back in the chair, deliberately obscene with my cock jutting out of my trousers, albeit gradually softening. It's shiny with her saliva. "Have I plugged it and then fucked your pussy and played with your clit until you grip my cock so hard as you come you milk my balls dry?"

Her cheeks tinge pink. "No."

"What about the first time I've sprayed come all over your breasts? Have you given me that first yet?"

"No." The word is breathy.

"What about your face? Have I covered that with come? Or fucked you from behind with your pert little bottom in the air? I haven't pushed you over my desk and filled you with my cock. I haven't tied your hands and feet together and gagged you, then screwed you while you're my helpless toy."

She gasps and licks her lips. They're plump and rosy from me fucking her mouth.

"I haven't chased you through the forest and held you down and fucked you as you beg for mercy, making you come over and over. I haven't pushed you to your knees and shoved my massive cock into your throat, making your eyes water. And if you think that you'll get away without sitting on my face, me holding your arse, you playing with your tits as I force you to orgasm when you believe you can't take more pleasure, when you say that one more will break you, you're so very, very wrong."

The subtle press of her legs together even as she doesn't reply makes me smirk. Such a demure little whore. She'll be the perfect wife.

"You should have known that this was not going to be one quick fumble in the dark, on your back, where you could think of England. Every first time I have from you will be depraved and leave you boneless with pleasure."

With slow deliberation, I recover my cock then rise to my feet.

"We can get started on all that as soon as you want, little bunny. Or we can do things *my* way."

"Your way?" She blinks nervously.

I catch her small hand in mine. "Yes."

11

WILLOW

"What are we doing?" I ask as he leads me upstairs. He slows his naturally longer gait to my shorter one, not tugging ahead.

"A shower, then sleep," he replies, tone full of amusement. "It's been a long day."

I don't know whether I'm disappointed or relieved that we won't be doing any of the tummy-fluttering things he suggested tonight. But my shoulders relax for a different reason that is more difficult to admit.

I won't have to leave if I give in to the sparks between Zane and me. There are many more firsts.

Trusting him feels good. Being near him is like home. I shouldn't give in to this, but I'm not sure I can stop myself. Zane says I'll be addicted to him by the time he's done everything he wants to me, but that's not what I'm worried about.

Nope.

My fear is, if I'm this in love with him after half a day, what will happen after a week? Or a month? Or however long it takes for Zane's imagination or interest in me to wane?

With every touch I fall for him more.

12

ZANE

She walks out of the bathroom as fresh and pink and sweet as a summer rose, far quicker than I expected, and I still only have a towel around my waist having showered in the ensuite next door.

Willow is wearing little pyjama shorts that reveal her legs, and a top with tiny straps. Her nipples are clearly visible. My cock responds immediately.

"You have tattoos," she murmurs.

I struggle with the instinct to put on a shirt as she approaches. I'm covered in tattoos and scars, and tattoos that cover uglier scars. Her looking at my naked chest is revealing the dark crevices of my past, and I don't want to scare her.

"You have a tree tattoo? Or is it a bush?"

"A mulberry," I explain in a low voice. It covers a nasty scar from the fight that made me a kingpin. "It's an emblem of Bethnal Green. I had it done when I took over the territory."

"Oh, they all have meanings?" She gets this curious look

in her eyes. Green eyes to go with my territory. As though I needed more signs that this was meant to be.

"Yeah."

"What are these?" She points at the mulberry fruits and skeleton hands that run down both my arms.

There is no nakedness like someone asking about your tattoos. "Each fruit represents one of my brothers."

"You have brothers?" She tilts her head like she can't imagine it.

"Had. They weren't biological brothers. They were my friends." I swallow. "I killed them all. There was a difficult transition when the former kingpin was murdered. Not by me," I hasten to say, an old twinge of hurt in my heart, no more than an echo now. "Shane Bethnal was like a father."

"*Like* a father?" Her gaze flicks between examining my body with something like fascination, and looking up into my eyes. "Not your actual father?"

I point at my side.

"Smith?" She runs her hands over the gothic lettering.

"I'm an orphan." Is it shameful to admit that? Perhaps, but Willow's face just pinches with sympathy, not disgust. "It was my surname because they couldn't think of anything else. I was brought up in care."

"But now your surname is Bethnal? Did you marry—"

"No." I quickly cut her off and see relief in the set of her shoulders. Was my little bunny jealous? "I adopted the name when I took over the territory. But I didn't want to forget."

"I like that." Reaching out, she runs her hands over my upper arms, and continues to explore, circling me. There are some tattoos I'd really rather not explain, but I do. Detailing the kills and the deals, the small triumphs and the losses as I climbed my way up to where I am now.

"There's a blank here." She's made her way around and stands before me again, tracing the space over my heart. The dip of my sternum and most of my left pectoral is only covered with dark hair. No ink.

"I never found anything I want to put there," I tell her rawly. "Until now."

Her fingers stop moving, and she takes a breath, then pauses, as though she wants to speak.

"A tree would fit." I didn't know I was waiting for her. But it never felt right to get a tattoo in that spot, and now I know why. It's for my girl.

"Another mulberry?" she asks tentatively.

"I was thinking of a willow," I murmur. "With a pair of animals under it." I push my hand into her hair, and she moans as I lower my head, breathing in her sweet strawberry scent. "Maybe a wolf and a little bunny."

Leaning forwards, I press a kiss onto her sleek hair. "I want to breed you, like the little bunny you are. One baby, then another. Then a third, a fourth."

Her lips part, but there's hope in her eyes as she gazes up at me.

"Do you want that? A big family that we love and raise?"

She nods eagerly. "I've always felt like it should have been like that for me, but..."

"Same." I never had a family, and she, for all that she's a Maldon and had three brothers, didn't either. "We'll have a family who is cherished and protected."

Deliberately, I run my hand down her side, familiarising myself with every inch of her. "I want to know you better than you know yourself. I'm obsessed with you, Willow."

I almost kiss her mouth, but fuck, as I'm a whisper away from her lips, I remember. Firsts. Only firsts.

For now.

So instead of devouring her as I'd like to, I put a hand to her back and tip her onto the bed. She shrieks and giggles as she bounces on the mattress, then stares up at me, taking me in as I discard the towel.

"I always sleep naked." But I don't always lower myself onto the bed with a hard-on that could break diamonds.

She bites her lip and doesn't take her eyes off me as I pull back the covers and let her wriggle underneath.

A soft huff of amusement stops me as I'm about to join her.

"What's so amusing, little bunny?" I say severely. No man wants his naked body laughed at.

"Nothing," she says, faking innocence.

I raise one eyebrow.

"It's just..." She pauses and rakes her gaze over my chest again. "I thought earlier that you couldn't look more attractive than you did in that suit." Her mouth stretches into a wry smile. "Totally wrong."

"Careful. You wouldn't want to swell my... Ego any more."

"It might explode," she replies. My naughty minx.

I slide into bed and pull her into my arms.

"I like this side of you," she whispers.

"The rough side?" My scars and tattoos are hardly attractive for a sweet thing like her.

"Relaxed. Funny. Telling me about yourself. Real," she says with a blush. "Though I like it when you take charge too."

I tangle my fingers in her hair. It's warm silk. "Both sides are real, little bunny."

She sighs contentedly.

"First time I've seen a man naked." Her gaze dips again to my chest.

Fuck. I am a fuckwit. I have made this impossible for myself, and wasted a first on getting into bed with her. Am I only going to see Willow naked once, too?

As I wrestle with what I can possibly say, her eyelids droop closed like a sleepy kitten, until she gives in, and her breathing is deep and even.

Watching her sleep—so beautiful, so young, so innocent —a sheen of guilt emerges onto my skin. I am not good enough. I shouldn't have made this devil of a bargain with her, she had no choice at all.

But every breath is the scent of strawberries, and looking at her...

There wasn't any option for me either.

I have to find a way to make her want to stay.

Something. Anything.

And I have an idea. Pulling my phone from the bedside table, I put my plan into action. Half an hour later, I've done what's needed and toss my phone back in favour of holding my sleeping girl with both arms.

She won't get away from me.

13

WILLOW

There's a low, regular thumping sound beneath my warm cheek. I'm held securely, surrounded by the scent of sandalwood and musk. I breathe it in like an addict.

Zane. His big arm is over my waist, and my head rests on his shoulder. It takes me a moment to realise that overnight I've snuggled into him and my face is next to his.

Another first. I spent the night with someone. I awoke feeling cherished. That's never happened before.

Not moving, I take my time looking at my captor, the man who owns the rights to every first. In sleep, he's even more ridiculously handsome.

"Mmm." His satisfied rumble alerts me that he's awake just quickly enough that I look really guilty when his eyes snap open. Zane grips me at the waist and pulls me right over his naked, hot, hard body. My legs part instinctively and I'm straddling him as he smirks up at me from below, his erection pressing up onto my clit.

Arousal starbursts through me. There's a layer of fabric between us—my pyjama shorts—but that does nothing to stop the sensation. Or the connection.

"Good morning," he murmurs, blue eyes sparkling.

"Morning." I squirm right onto where he's hard.

Zane repeats the motion, and I grasp his chest for support.

"You like that, huh? Go on." Reaching up, he squeezes my breast possessively. "A morning orgasm is a delicious indulgence. Use me. Rub your little cunt on me and make yourself come this way. For the first time."

He rolls his hips upwards, and I gasp as pleasure sparks from where we touch. It's as though the arousal never receded from last night, and all it takes is Zane's filthy words and him working me over his cock, and it flares back. My clit is super-sensitive, and I'm already almost cross-eyed with lust.

"Don't worry," he croons. "I'll find new ways to make you come every morning."

He shifts his hands down to my hips and moves me, rubbing my clit over his rigid length.

"Just ask me the night before, and I'll show you what a fantastic way to wake orgasming is. I'll lick you until you open your eyes as you come, squirting over my face."

I flush as I imagine it and he keeps playing me on him. Every part is a different sort of hot and delicious. Squirting? So embarrassing. But if he liked it, or if he teased me, I think I'd be proud to come that way. And him licking me as I slept? A shimmer goes down my spine. The idea of being woken by Zane between my legs, doing whatever he liked, is obscene and should make me feel powerless. And yet now he's said it, I need it. Desperately.

Just like in the forest, I'm ludicrously turned on when Zane takes control.

"You're so wet for me," he groans.

And he's right. I've soaked through my pyjama bottoms

and that's making this easy. That and the fact Zane is urging me on, almost forcing this onto me. I don't need to say yes or no, he's doing it, and it feels amazing.

"Willow." He drags me roughly back and forth as he grinds up. "Fuck you're..." His fingers bite into my hips and the pain heightens the pleasure. "Perfect."

I'm caught up in my own arousal, and it takes a second for me to realise what's happening. He pulses beneath my open pussy, but his blue eyes remain open, staring up at me even as they go hazy, and his jaw clenches and he groans.

I glance down.

His abdomen is streaked with white liquid, and I can't take in what it means for a second.

Then I get it, as he shudders beneath me, still rocking me on his length, sending flares of bliss up and down my spine. He came. It takes him a second to catch his breath, and mine disappears, because there's something so unrestrained and feral about how he used my body to tip him over, while also rubbing my clit in a way that is overwhelming.

"Look what a mess you made," he teases and wipes the liquid from his sculpted, ink-covered abs, the trail of dark hair that leads to his cock now flattened, and brings it up to my breast.

I watch, speechless, as he tugs down my Cami top and smears his come onto my breasts.

"Filthy," he purrs, then grabs my side, pulling me down to him and the next second, his mouth is on my nipple, laving it, pulsing ecstasy to my core. Then he bites, and at the same time, pulls me over him rubbing my clit at a new angle, and it's too much. The shock of him painting me with his release, and my body's response to it, plus the attention on my breasts, tips me over.

I sob as pleasure radiates through me.

"My god, Zane," I choke out as my pussy clenches in orgasm. It's satisfying, and yet it's immediately not enough. I need more, and I crave something to anchor and fill me. Him.

"I know, I know." He's comforting me, but I hardly comprehend why.

I haven't recovered my brain from where it migrated to between my legs when Zane sweeps the covers away and lifts me out of bed, still plastered to his chest. Wordlessly, he takes me to the bathroom and it's under the warm water of the shower, completely naked, that I fully come to.

"You're so sexy, you know that?" he says as he slides me down his body to stand on my own wobbly legs. He makes an impatient noise when I attempt to clean myself, so I just... Give in. I let him turn me this way and that, washing me like I'm his doll.

As I dress in a pair of denim shorts and a T-shirt, I peek at him buttoning a dark grey shirt over those revealing tattoos. And after he's efficiently in a full suit and left me with a promise to be back when he's fixed us breakfast, I fuss with my hair, putting it up, then brushing it down twice before I leave it down. Zane said he liked my hair. It's always a good thing to please your kidnapper, right?

But it's not that. I just want him to like me, I admit in the privacy of my own head. What if I could be so good, he'd continue to believe he loves me?

I don't even get lost on the way down to the kitchen. This house just makes sense to me. It shouldn't, but maybe I'm done with fighting what feels right.

So when Zane has coffee and lemon drizzle cake spread ready for me on the table, I can't help myself. I impulsively go to him, boosting onto my tiptoes.

"Thank you," and I try to kiss his cheek. He's far too tall for that without his cooperation though, so I see the full effect of his stunned expression, making me fear I've misjudged this.

"Sorry, I—" But that's as far as I get with that sentence before he's leaned down, wrapped his arms around my waist and lifted me off my feet. Then he's kissing me with a hungry mouth that tastes of black coffee.

Electricity shoots through my veins. Zane is all the caffeine fix I need.

14

ZANE

She tried to kiss me. *She* kissed me back.

Fuck, my heart is so light, it might fly away.

I hold her tight with one arm—her feet must be dangling a foot off the ground but neither of us care—and lace my other hand into her soft dark hair. I kiss her for indulgent minutes, angling our mouths together. She clings to me, arms around my shoulders, and her enthusiasm for our third kiss is better than anything I've ever felt. I'd give up forty years of life for this perfect moment.

It's only when I hear my phone ping that I realise I've messed up. My bunny is such a distraction.

Not letting her go, I carry her with me, kissing her as she laughs and questions my sanity as I dump our drinks into travel cups and pass her the piece of lemon drizzle cake. I'm glad my staff arranged that as I ordered.

"Where are we going?" she asks as we get outside to where the helicopter is waiting again.

"To Bethnal Green. I've got something for you."

15

WILLOW

I grip his arm as he guides me, one big hand over my eyes, one at my back. We turn, and sunshine falls onto my bare legs.

"Ready?" he rumbles from behind me. Zane insisted on covering my eyes as we entered, and while allowing a mafia boss to blind you sounds like a bad thing, I'm throwing all my preconceptions out. Zane isn't like my family. He brought me my favourite cake, after all.

"Born ready," I lie, and he huffs at my poor joke then lifts his hand.

It takes my sight a second to adjust.

We're in a big, open room, lined with empty wooden bookshelves on three sides, and a large window that's obscured. There's a high ceiling with an old, round skylight, and fancy borders and flower patterns in the white plaster. The floor is dark, shiny wood boards.

"Do you like it?" Zane asks from behind me, and I swear there's apprehension in his voice.

"I love it," I breathe. And I do. It's got so much potential. "What is it?"

"It's your bookshop."

I spin around and gape at him.

"There are still a few things needed," he adds. "A counter, more shelves. Tables, I think?"

My mind fills in the blanks, and I imagine the room with book displays, and colourful banners.

"And stock of books, of course. That leads to Bethnal high street." He gestures to where the windows are obscured with opaque film. "You could have a reading nook there, with cosy chairs?"

This is amazing. Better than I could ever have imagined, and I have been daydreaming about my bookshop since I was old enough to love books.

Disappointment twists in me. "How can I fund it?"

"Shops make money, no?" he replies dryly.

I want to make my bookshop outstanding. The place of my dreams, that would do this building justice, and that needs investment before any customers step inside. "Yes, but—"

"All the setup will be paid for by me," Zane cuts me off.

"A debt." My stomach dips. I know about mafia debts.

"A gift," he corrects softly, then the corner of his mouth tugs up. "Though if you want to give me something in return, I won't complain."

"You won't complain, huh?" I can't help but smile back. "What were you thinking of?" My mind goes to the feel of his cock at the back of my throat and him losing control. I wouldn't mind that again. I enjoyed seeing him overcome, helpless with pleasure that I gave him.

He steps forward and draws me gently into his arms, hands at my waist. I look up into his handsome face, and remember his expression as he came without even any direct contact between us this morning. He looks as intense now as he did coming apart as he moved me over his cock.

"What about a baby?" he says, low and dark.

I'm shocked all over again, and a frisson of arousal flicks to my core. I didn't really think he was serious when he said yesterday he wanted children.

"Is that one of the firsts you're claiming?" I'm not sure if I want it to be, or not. Maybe I want him to say it's non-negotiable. Or would it be sweeter if this was just a gift between us, no deals?

He's unreadable as he tilts his head. "It could be."

"Why?"

"Why do I want to breed you?" His eyes go soft and intent at the same time. "I should think that's obvious."

Oh. My mouth goes dry, and my body is suddenly brittle. Just a mafia thing, after all. "An heir."

He laughs. "No, not that."

Raising his hands, he sweeps my hair back as though he's going to make a ponytail, then tugs. My chin tilts up. I'm his puppet.

"I want to give you a baby because I want to have you entirely, without limits," he rumbles, looking down with those white-blue-heat eyes and I melt like he's a blowtorch. "Taking you raw, and filling you up would be ecstasy. I'd like to fuck you bareback, nothing between us, until you're overflowing."

I can't breathe. But not in a bad way. More like, if I move at all, maybe he'll stop saying these things and I couldn't bear that.

"My fertile little bunny, I want us to have a dozen kids. I want to plant my seed deep inside you and watch it grow. I'd love to see you swollen and fertile."

"And the bookshop?" I say. "Why the bookshop? Just

to trade for a baby?" The doubt is instinctive. There's a voice in my head from my family that says a mafia princess doesn't do anything as lowering as work in a bookshop. And nothing good in my life has ever been without a cost I wasn't willing to pay. An offer of two things that I want—a baby and a bookshop—must have a catch.

"No," he says harshly. "Never that."

Taking my face between his palms he looks into my eyes, and despite everything, I think there's honesty in the kingpin's severe expression.

"Because I believe in you, and your vision for what a bookshop can be. I think this will be a fantastic resource for Bethnal. You'll fill it with joy and knowledge and escapism."

It's a good thing he's holding my head, because otherwise it might just fall off. He doesn't think it would be a bad thing for me to do. He sounds not just accepting of my idea, but proud. Supportive.

My heart squeezes. "Really?"

"Of course." He nods seriously. "And I want to make you happy."

That steals my breath. No one has ever said that to me before. In fact, I don't think anyone has ever cared in the slightest about my happiness, or my opinions, or anything but what I could do for them.

"Zane..." I don't know who moves—him towards me or me backwards drawing him with me—but my bottom hits the desk. Then he has bumped me onto it, and his fist is in my hair, and he forces his way between my knees.

"Willow," he murmurs. "Say something. Because if you don't, and you keep looking at me like that, I'm going to take it as an invitation."

Do I want him to? I can't stop staring at him, that's for

sure. The big scary kingpin who listened to me, and gave me cake and a bookshop.

His tattoos aren't visible right now, but the recollection of them echoes through me. All the years of experience and work and hardship that they represent. And that space on his chest, as though his heart has never been given away. I can't help but wonder if I could snuggle into that gap on his chest, as he said.

This one day has changed my life. I'm comfortable in a way that I never have been before. I don't have a gap in my tattoos, but I did have an emptiness. It's only now Zane has filled it with affection and trust that I've noticed how it's not painful anymore. It's not an open wound.

Anyone who cared for me would say I was being reckless by trusting a London Mafia Boss. But that's the point, isn't it? None of my family really cares, and the restrictive life of a mafia princess has meant I don't have friends.

And the thing is, I think Zane's right. We belong together. It's some bone-deep primal recognition.

He runs his hand up my arm and over my shoulder to my neck, lightly clasping me there, but the power it holds rocks me.

Would it be so bad to give in?

"Tell me," he says hoarsely. "I need to hear you say—"

A harsh knock on the door reverberates through the room.

We both freeze.

"Our first customer?" I joke, but something about this isn't right. Zane's brow goes dark.

"Bethnal," comes a man's voice. It's posh and authoritative.

Zane closes his eyes and grits his teeth. "Not now, Westminster."

Westminster. He's the leader of the London Mafia Syndicate. It's a big, powerful organisation, and the Essex Cartel's enemy.

Dread crawls down my spine. This cannot be anything good.

"We're here to negotiate the return of your captive."

16

ZANE

Shit.

Looking into Willow's face, there are flickering emotions. Fear, worry.

"Open the door, Bethnal, before Westminster gets impatient and does stupid things." Mayfair's Russian accent has all the grace of a rusty chainsaw.

I shift my hand to cup her cheek. It's totally covered by my palm. She's so delicate and tiny.

"Bethnal!" Westminster this time. "Don't make me break down the door."

"Alright, calm yourselves," I call, not looking away from Willow's face.

She blinks up at me, her lips parting.

"I'm not letting you go," I tell her. "Do you understand?"

I'm being harsh, but I don't care.

She nods, and I have to accept that as enough.

"Thank god, I'm too old for shouldering my way through solid objects," Westminster says as I unlock the door and swing it open. "And shooting the lock would make a mess on this nice vintage—"

"The answer is no," I interrupt him.

Artem, the kingpin of Mayfair, sighs. "She's here, da?"

"Yes," I grit out.

"Her brothers want to talk to her, and negotiate with you," says Westminster.

"Well, you can all fuck off. That is rather how kidnapping works." She's mine.

"And then you talk to someone about the price of their family member's return." Westminster shakes his head like I'm being deliberately difficult.

"You only met her yesterday, so this isn't about her, is it?" Mayfair says.

They don't understand. This is *all* about Willow. There are soft footsteps across the room from where I left my girl straightening her clothes after I nearly mauled her.

"Be civilised and demand the ransom, Bethnal." Westminster states this as though it's the only ending he can imagine.

"I have everything I want." I reach my hand backwards without looking, and for a second, I think she's going to leave me hanging. Then Willow's palm slides over mine, soft and warm. I interlock our fingers and give them a little squeeze to say, *Good girl.*

Neither of the two mafia bosses miss the gesture, and they exchange a look.

"Fun fact, Artem and I met because of a hostage situation. You might become friends with the Maldons," Westminster says.

"I do not need a fucking bromance," I snap. Brother-in-laws, maybe. But after hearing about the ways they have controlled and kept her down, I'm not very inclined to spend time with Willow's family.

"It's not a bromance," they say in perfect unison, and Willow smothers a laugh.

"It is a bromance," says a woman, strolling up, eyes twinkling.

"I told you to wait, darling, because it's dangerous." Westminster pulls the woman under his arm with a scowl.

Snuggling into him, the woman regards Willow and me curiously.

"I'm Anwyn, Ben's wife. And you should definitely come to this meeting," she chirps. "You might start a maths club together."

"I don't know why you think that would be appealing," I reply, my irritation seeping into my voice. My gaze flicks towards the street. My men are there, of course. They let Mayfair and Westminster past because they're allies of Bethnal Green. I can't blame them for this shitshow.

"I hear it's popular," Mayfair deadpans.

"Not. Maths," I bite out. "For fuck's sake you guys already expect me to keep count of how many people I've killed, and now you want to mess up a debt collection. Witham owed me."

"Do we collect murder stats?" Mayfair asks Westminster, ignoring my second point.

"Just for baselining purposes. I thought it would be good to have an idea of the trend and aim for death reduction in future years."

"No, I draw the line there." Mayfair shakes his head firmly. "Ben, that's too far. We are not actually a maths club or a government."

"Well then, I guess the kidnapping is fine," Westminster huffs impatiently. "And we don't object to Bethnal's little private security thing he has going on. It's like the bloody 1950s, but the Bobbies have tattoos."

Mayfair shakes his head, baffled. "Do you mean boobies?"

"No, Bobbies." Westminster sighs. "It's an old-fashioned name for the police, dating back to the founding of the force by—"

"Will you be standing around discussing history when the bookshop is open, and I hit you over the head with a history hardback?" I snap. This is enough. "Why are you still here?"

"Her family approached me about resolving this." Westminster folds his arms and his gaze flicks between Willow, our joined hands, and my face. "The London Mafia Syndicate was founded to resolve kidnap situations more amicably. And although I admit we've branched out—"

"Into fucking mathematics and road maintenance," Mayfair grumbles.

"The welfare of vulnerable young people remains a core part of our organisation." Westminster doesn't pause, speaking over Mayfair.

It's for Willow's good that I'm not allowing her family near her. "I'm not meeting with—"

"You are, it's not even worth the argument, Bethnal." Anwyn's bright voice cuts in, and there's silence.

I look down at Willow beside me, wordlessly asking her opinion.

"It can't hurt to hear them out?" she whispers.

It absolutely can. I don't trust those fuckers. They'll try to manipulate this situation. But so long as I keep Willow, anything else is sacrificial.

"Fine."

We meet in a restaurant where the outskirts of London slide into the Essex territory. Westminster has snarled at me four times that I didn't need to do my own checks, and that there was no way things could go wrong because only he and Mayfair are armed.

I sent more men.

It's only when Turner has had enough too, asking if I want him to build a concrete bunker while he's at it, that I allow Willow in. It's an old pub, low ceiling, black painted beams, stone floor, and dark wood chairs with brass domes holding on flower patterned fabric. There are lots of people dining, and only a few look up as we walk in. They're all eating lunch, casually taking their lives in their hands.

The three Maldon men are waiting, sitting in a line around a third of a round table.

"Willow, are you okay?" one says as we approach.

"I'm fine, Wesley," she replies tightly, and takes the seat one away from her brother, leaving a gap. I sling my arm over her shoulders as I take the seat furthest, and Mayfair sits next to me. On his other side sit Westminster and his wife, again allowing a space between them and the Maldons.

There's a glint of black metal out of the corner of my eye as Mayfair settles in his chair. His gun, holstered on his left hip—he must be left-handed—is quickly covered by his suit jacket.

"You screwed with a very lucrative deal for us, Bethnal," the middle of the Maldon men says. He was at the front of the church, promising to pay Witham's debts. Robert. He has the vibe of being the eldest, and used to being in charge.

I send him a death stare that would make any of my

men cower because they'd know what it meant. Robert isn't so smart.

I open my mouth to say that I'll offer whatever they want, then stop. Will that upset Willow if I—in effect—bought her? I regard her profile.

"The loss of the Witham territory, and the damage to the Maldon reputation after that stunt you pulled at the wedding have cost us a lot," Robert continues, and names a ludicrous figure. "And the cost of our sister's potential auction price since she isn't marrying Witham. That's about half as much again."

"You think Willow is worth less than the Witham territory?" I enquire. Willow looks down, silent and subdued. I suspect the issue of her value is important. I cannot fuck this up.

"That's just the price of bitch—"

"Don't call her that," I growl. I won't have my girl insulted.

"She's our sister," Robert replies, curling his lip. "We'll call her whatever we want."

"Not in front of me." I've raised my voice, and a couple of diners glance around nervously. "Or you'll regret it."

"Miss Maldon will be treated with respect while we're all at this table," Westminster interjects in moderate tones.

"We want our sister back," says the quieter of the three Maldon men.

Willow snorts.

I toy with a tendril of her hair, curling it on my finger until it locks and tugs. She tips her head just an inch, and the sensation of ownership of her is potent. She's mine. I'm not giving her up.

"Why do you want her?" I suspect I'm not going to like the answer.

"Look, it's like this," the other Maldon brother breaks in as Robert starts to speak.

"Who are you?" I snap.

"That's Liam," Willow says quietly.

This nervous girl version of her is unacceptable. I'd rather have the one who ran from me. The one who came for me. The one who was brave and sweet and sexy.

"Maldon needed the Witham territory to stay afloat, and powerful in Essex. And we need all our resources, including the value of Willow as a bride, or at auction."

"Auction?" I ask, and Willow huddles further into herself.

"Virgin auction," Liam clarifies.

"What if I told you that wasn't possible anymore?" I reply softly. Willow turns to me, wide-eyed. I glance across, reassuring her with my eyes. All her firsts. I might not have taken her virginity yet, but I'm not allowing anyone else to touch her. Ever.

"You little whore—" Robert hisses, eyes blazing and hands slapping on the table.

"Take that back." My words are a low, dangerous snarl. One of the Maldon brothers recognises it for the threat it is, recoiling, but the other two don't.

"What makes you think he'll—" Her eldest brother doesn't know when to shut up, so I stop him mid-sentence.

"I'm telling you to *take it back.*" I can't pretend not to be angry, and my hand has tightened in Willow's hair.

"She's *my* whore of a sister. You stupid cunt," Robert spits.

"I'm warning you not to insult my wife again."

"Your wife?" Liam exclaims this time, whereas everyone else just gapes at Willow and me. Though not Willow, who has gone utterly still at my announcement, and her gaze has dipped to her lap.

"And I'm telling you she's not your wife," Robert says.

"My future wife." I lean down and whisper into her ear, "All your firsts, remember little bunny. I'll be your husband too."

"You want her? Pay," says Wesley.

Finally, some fucking sense. I'm okay with this if Willow is, but I can't see her face, so I'm not sure.

"He won't cough up what she's worth at auction," grumbles Liam.

"Not for damaged goods," Robert sneers, and Willow flinches.

"It was your idea to marry her off," Wesley points out. "You can't blame her for taking a better option."

"I don't know why you're so keen to defend her," Robert says in an undertone not meant for my ears, but I hear it anyway. "She always was a disloyal bitch."

And my anger explodes this time. It's uncontrollable.

I snatch Artem's gun from its holster and have it armed and fired before Robert can breathe another word.

A split second of his shocked expression, then he slumps forward. Dead.

"Fuck!" Westminster is on his feet and has his gun trained on Wesley Maldon before he's even finished that exclamation.

Someone screams. Several people, I think.

Liam lunges for Willow and I fire again as he reaches out. My bunny squeaks and jolts back against my chest as he too falls. The headshot means he's lost all capacity to touch her before he even hits the table.

"Bethnal. What was that?" Westminster demands.

"I warned them," I reply without looking, dropping a

kiss onto the top of Willow's head, gaze fixed on her one alive brother on the far side of the two slumped dead in their chairs. "I told them not to insult my girl."

Mayfair sighs and Westminster's wife lets out what I suspect is a snort of amusement. I ignore them. Willow is trembling under my arm.

"I'm not as restrained as Westminster here." I point my gun at Wesley. "I'll kill you without any question."

"No need." His voice wobbles, but he lifts his chin.

"You can have the Witham territory." I don't give a shit, and Turner will be delighted to not have to deal with that snake pit. So long as I have Willow, and she's safe, anything else is on the table. It always was.

To my side, Westminster rumbles with discontent. That prick is thinking of the wider advantage of the London Mafia Syndicate, not realising I'd throw them all off a cliff to save Willow.

"Shut up," I mutter at Westminster, and to be fair to him, he does.

Wesley Maldon's expression hardens. "And safe passage."

"This is what is going to happen," I say in a hard voice. "You will leave your sister here, in my care, and never touch or hurt her again. You return to Maldon. You tell your family and the Essex Cartel that your brothers fucked up by messing with Bethnal. You take over the Witham territory, and you secretly feed information to me about the Essex Cartel, or I will come after you. And I will not be as merciful to an unarmed man as Westminster is."

He looks for a second like he might argue.

"And you are never going to insult my wife—" Willow hiccups. "—My *future* wife, again. Do you understand?"

Wesley's mouth twists in distaste as he glances down at his two dead brothers. "They were dicks anyway."

"Leave before I change my mind." I tighten my grip on my girl. I want him away from Willow.

"Have a nice life, sis," he tosses over to her as he stands and walks away. And although it's unfeeling for a brother, and he doesn't look back, it has a ring of sincerity under the flippant words.

There's absolute silence apart from the jarringly soothing piano music. Everyone in the pub is looking at us.

"Could I have my gun back now?" Mayfair asks, holding out his hand casually.

"Thank you for the loan," I reply, placing it on the table before him.

"It was theft—"

"It was a diplomatic disaster," snaps Westminster.

"As if you'd put up with anyone insulting me," his wife, Anwyn, snorts.

Westminster holsters his gun with an irritated sigh and pulls her into his arms, muttering, "Fine."

Against my chest, Willow begins to shake.

I need to get her out of here. "Could you—"

"Yes, we'll deal with these," Mayfair says, indicating the corpses of Willow's brothers.

I scoop Willow into my arms, carrying her bridal style. Again.

Kidnapping her. Again.

17

WILLOW

He killed two of my brothers.

I should definitely care, but as Zane barks orders to his men who group around us, I don't.

They never gave a toss about me, but Zane wouldn't stand by as they insulted me, even though it was mild compared to what they've said and done in the past. And I love that he defended me.

I love *him*.

The realisation hits me and my god, but it's a warm bubble expanding from my chest. I love him.

Zane sets me down at the door, and we walk into the street together. His arm around my waist brooks no argument, but he shortens his stride to accommodate me. We round a corner and there's a railings and bushes enclosed garden, right in the centre of rows of houses, and there's the swirl of helicopter blades from inside the little park.

"Zane," I begin, but I'm not sure what to say. Thank you? Where are we going? Can we go home? Did you really mean it that you want to marry me?

I want you to be my husband.

He told my brothers I was his wife, like it was a predestined thing.

I love you.

"No," he says, voice gruffer than I've heard it. "Get in, Willow. Now."

18

ZANE

There's no privacy for talking in the helicopter, and thankfully Willow doesn't argue, allowing me to buckle her into a seat. A short time later, we're back at the house in Suffolk and the helicopter has spun off into the sky after we walk away.

I slow to a stop on the lawn and Willow does too, looking at me with an expression of surprise as we stand in the warm afternoon sunlight.

"This is your last chance, Willow," I say tightly. "If you don't want to be mine, you need to speak right now." Otherwise, I'm taking murdering her brothers as a sign that she's happy to stay.

"You just gave up the Witham territory," she whispers, her brows puckering with confusion.

I shrug. It was never about that. All this was only ever for her.

She takes a tentative step closer and it's all I can do not to lift her into my arms again.

I hold off.

"You know those ethical dilemmas?" I reply instead,

because she has to know all of it. "The ones where you have, say, a big family about to be hit by a train, and a person you could sacrifice to save the children?"

She nods, but looks uncertain.

"If you were the one person, I'd let them die," I say roughly. "I'd go over there and throw them in front of the train myself."

That makes her draw in breath.

"I'd send millions into fire if I could have one more minute with you."

Her gulp shows I'm making my point.

"Do not mistake me, I am a bad, bad man." I grab her chin between my thumb and forefinger, tilting her head to force her to look into my eyes. "I killed your brothers. I am obsessed with you already. It will get worse. I am unhinged. I'll never be reasonable about you, and your safety, and I guess that's a red flag, or whatever people on the internet say.

"But I am *your* bad man," I add more softly. "I will care for you, and I will love you. So long as there is breath in my body, I will put myself between you and any harm or threat."

"Zane, I—"

"You can leave if you want," I cut her off, because if I don't make this promise aloud, now, I might not have the resolve to follow through. "I'll take you somewhere else, that's safe. And we can both pretend I don't watch you, and stalk you, and kill any man who touches you."

She shakes her head slowly, and my stomach plunges.

I continue anyway.

"I won't give you up completely, but if freedom is really what you want—or the illusion of it at least—you have to tell me before I claim you and can't let you go."

It causes physical pain to drop my hand away. But I want a wife, not a prisoner. Either she feels the same, or she—

The air is knocked out of me as Willow throws herself against my chest. My arms close over her instinctively, and she clings, having somehow got her hands over my shoulders, and wrapped her legs around my waist.

"Little bunny." I squeeze her, dragging in the strawberry scent of her hair. "Mine. You're mine."

"I love you," she whispers into my neck.

For a second, I'm not sure I've heard right, but my heart takes it in anyway, jumping and expanding. I pull back her head so I can see her face.

"Say it again." I must look ferocious, manic.

But Willow just smiles. "I tried to fight it, but there's no point."

"No, there isn't." I tighten my grip on her arse and her hair. "You're my soulmate. You can't escape me, and anyone who takes you from me will pay with their life."

I'm moving then, taking her into the house with one thought in my lizard brain: get her to a bed. Get inside her. Breed her. Make her mine in every way, forever.

"Good," she replies, then deliberately pulls up against my hold. It must tug her hair, and she lets out a sound of pleasure-pain as our mouths touch.

And that's it.

I take the stairs two at a time and crash through the door to our bedroom. Kissing her, my tongue thrusting into her mouth, I lower her to the bed and cover her with my body.

Being with Willow and having my lips on hers is like coming home after a lifetime in exile, but I'm impatient for more. I grab at her clothes, tugging them to get at her naked skin.

"Have to see you. Now," I grit out, my hands all over her. Then there's no patience left in me, and I rip all the fabric I can reach, even as I keep kissing her.

She squeaks with surprise, but doesn't complain as I drag the tatters of her top and shorts off her. I rear up, and the fact she's still wearing knickers is un-fucking-welcome. Willow is trying to get my clothes off too, so far achieving only my tie and three middle buttons with her less efficient but not as destructive methods.

I grab the cotton panties in both hands and tear them from her body, leaving her naked.

"Spread your legs," I demand, and though she obeys, it's not quickly enough and I shove them roughly apart, my hands on her knees and reveal a sight that makes me groan.

"Fuck, look at you. My priceless jewel." She's pink and shiny. So soft and tempting. "You're going to taste like heaven, and I can't wait to eat your pussy until you come on my face."

"Please, Zane. Let me touch you." She reaches for me but I'm not sure I've got enough control to keep myself together and make this as perfect for her as it has to be if she's exploring with her soft little hands.

"Soon, soon," I promise, catching her hand and kissing the palm. "But before that, you're going to be a good girl and come for me."

"Zane!" she protests. "I don't need that, I need your—"

"Willow," I cut her off in my sternest voice. "This is your first time, and I have to do it right."

"Now, I just want you *now*." Frustration laces her words.

"Don't make me force you to be good," I warn her lightly. "I only have so much control, little bunny."

That stops her, and makes her bite her lip. Then, slowly, deliberately, she sits up and nudges at my suit jacket.

"Like that, is it?" I grab her wrist with one hand, and my tie from where she discarded it on the bed with the other. In seconds I've bound the soft dark-red silk around her wrists and eased them over her head.

I exhale, and look into her face as I discard the suit jacket, and flick open my top button. My knee is between her legs. "Better?"

"No," she mutters, but the way she arches her back, pushing tits up towards me, says, "Yes".

I smirk. "Don't worry, you will be." I run one hand down her front and pause on her flat belly. "I'm going to fuck a baby into there."

"Then do it!" she whines.

"When you're ready, little bunny," I reply. "And not before." Dipping my head, I kiss her inner thighs, teasing both of us. Her skin is soft and sweet. I kiss closer and closer, until I breathe in the scent of her pussy, and she shivers.

Then I take a long, decadent lick up her seam and groan. "You're delicious." I use my fingers to part her wet folds, and taste her again. She's sugar and musk and a little bit salty, and I cannot get enough of her, especially when she wriggles and sighs as I run my tongue over her clit.

I'd love to talk her through all this, but I'm incapable of doing anything but gorging on her. I alternate between holding her legs further apart and using my thumb to prepare her needy little hole.

There's no compromise. I don't say it aloud because I don't need to. My message is already clear: I'm not fucking you, little bunny, until you've come.

And I'm not stopping licking her either. I'm insistent.

Then I want more. I shift so I can hold her pussy lips fully open with one hand, and plunge a finger into her tight passage. She bows and gasps at the intrusion.

I don't apologise. I ram into her, rubbing upwards to where she's sensitive, feeling for the right spot and listening to her whimpers. As soon as she's given me enough space, I pull out and this time it's two fingers, and I find the place that makes her cry out with only a few more strokes.

Willow sobbing is the sweetest thing I've ever heard, and she quivers beneath my mouth and on my fingers, getting more and more wound up. And then I feel it before she vocalises her pleasure. She goes rigid, and her legs jerk.

She clenches around my fingers and the fierce, possessive pride in me is fire as she cries out in satisfaction. I kiss and lick her through it.

"So fucking perfect," I mutter against her clit as I ease off.

My cock is thick and desperate to claim Willow's virgin pussy, straining my trousers so hard I'm surprised it hasn't ripped a seam open. I want her pregnant with my child as soon as possible.

I look up. Her cheeks are flushed, and her long hair is messy where she's been thrashing around.

She looks thoroughly debauched. I smirk.

"*Now* you're ready to be bred."

19
___

WILLOW

You know when you leave a bar of chocolate in the sunshine, and it looks the same as it did before it was heated through, but when you touch it, it's all melted and squidgy?

That's me right now, and Zane is the sun.

I'm pretty sure I've been changed at a molecular level.

I've never felt anything as good as the white-hot pleasure from Zane licking me. He hasn't stopped, either. As though he loves the taste, he's running his tongue over my pussy lips, careful not to touch where I'm over sensitised.

But despite being liquid, I'm still desperate.

"Zane," I plead, and tug on my tied hands. Being helpless like this is spiralling up my desire. I thought goading him to make me his would drive him wild, and it has, but it's also brought out his stubborn streak. "I need you."

His eyes are sharp on me, his face in dark shadows. "What do you need, little bunny?"

"You. Please."

"Do you need me to fill you with my cock?" His hands go to his belt.

Impossibly, my clit twitches.

"Yes," I breathe.

I get a glimpse of strained fabric as he stands and rips open his trousers. My mouth waters at the sight of his cock, jutting upwards, large and proud. He strokes the length, eyes going hazy as he looks down at my ruined, sluttish self, lying on his bed completely naked.

"Will you come on my cock like a good girl if I fuck you?"

My pussy clenches. Empty, so empty.

"Yes."

"Do you want me to come deep inside you and plant my seed, so I give you a baby?" He raises one eyebrow.

He thinks he has to make me crazy to accept this. I know he's trying to get me to beg more. But here's the thing: two can play at the teasing game.

He's licked me until I'm mindless, but I rally my thoughts. I want him feral. I want him as undone as I am.

"Just here?" I writhe, arching my hips to indicate my belly. "Would you like to see me swollen with your child?"

And it's his turn to grit his teeth and moan.

"Tell me you'd like to have me pregnant with your baby." I push my shoulders into the mattress, offering up my breasts. "These would get all big and milky, too."

"Little fucking tease," he says hoarsely, taking me in with his hungry gaze.

I smile. "It'll work. Everyone will know I'm yours when I'm swollen and pregnant. When I give birth to a boy with dark hair and pale-blue eyes."

He groans and strokes his cock faster. The tip is reddening, and I swear it's bigger now.

"Would you like to suck my nipples then?"

I think I shocked him because he stops abruptly. I certainly just surprised myself. And for a full second, I'm scared I've made a miscalculation.

Then Zane grins. "Oh yes. There's nothing that will make me want you less. I'll steal a bit of milk from my infant, and fuck you until I have to put my hand over your mouth so you don't wake the baby as you scream in pleasure. I'll love and want you until the end of time, Willow."

My breasts tingle with anticipation. I believe him.

"Fuck me as you're meant to, Zane."

He rises up, and is on top of me in a second, fully clothed in contrast to my bared skin and ferocious, burning intensity that I want to have all over me. The slide of his shirt on my skin is a heated reminder of how he has power over me. I'm happy to hand over control because I trust him completely to give me what I didn't even know I needed.

I thought I wanted the freedom to choose. Turns out, it was love that was missing.

Then he lowers his head, and I get a glimpse of his wicked smile before he gets one of my nipples between his teeth and tugs mercilessly.

He doesn't kiss my breasts, he devours them. Just as when he was licking my pussy, he eats me whole. It's unlike anything I've experienced as he bites first one nipple then the other. It sends a bolt of arousal right down my torso.

I'm so overwhelmed by how he's worshipping my breasts, I barely notice him nudging my legs apart where they've fallen together. I'm writhing with pure desire, unable to do anything but lie and take what he gives me. And it borders on pain, it's so good, but every time he sucks too hard, he gentles up when I cry out. I'm so wound up. Despite all my fine thoughts about teasing him, Zane is utterly in control, his big body holding me down and the sting of his tie around my wrists.

I look at him, and blink as I notice the pink-red of a bruise on the swell of my breast.

"Fuck." He lets out a rumbling growl as he presses his lips to my skin again, then rears up. "You're so sexy. I can't wait any longer."

"You don't need to. Take me," I urge him.

He drags his shirt over his head and there's a rip as he takes the cuffs over his wrists, then shoving his trousers and underwear down in one and kicking off the whole lot without moving away from me. As though he needs us to be close as much as I do.

His cock is leaking pre-come, a white bead at the tip and dribbling down the curved head. My mouth waters.

I half want him to straddle me and feed me his cock right here, between my lips, and fuck my throat. But I need him between my legs more.

There's no ceremony as my tattooed and scar-covered lover—the kingpin of Bethnal Green—falls over me. He's so big in every way, and I'm tiny beneath him. The contrast of his patterned skin, with the roughness of the hair that trails down his middle, compared to my plainness sends an unexpected shudder of desire down my spine.

And that cock. I gasp as the hot, silky-smooth head of him touches my folds then nudges forward. I wish I could hold him to me, but equally I like that I only have one thing to focus on. All I have to do is accept him.

"I'm going to take your virginity now," he rasps. He's on his elbows, and shifts his hand to caress the side of my neck, running his palm up to my jaw, then over my lips. It's a shock when he slides two fingers into my mouth, so intimate even compared to our nakedness.

"Little bunny, bite down when I hurt you. I want to share every bit of pain, because fuck, I know your tight, wet, hot little pussy is going to be my heaven. Made for my pleasure."

He pushes into me.

I make mewling sounds like a wounded animal as he forces my body to accept his fat dick.

"That's it," he rumbles. "You're mine now."

It's only then I realise I've done as he asked, biting down on his fingers.

It hurts. There's no other word for it, but my god, it hurts like growing pains, like a caterpillar reforming into a butterfly. I let out a hiss, and Zane soothes me. I release my jaw as the sharpest pain dissipates, and turn my head to press kisses into his palm.

I close my eyes and for a long moment there's nothing but the way he's splitting me open. He's making space for himself in me, and it's like from the start. He realised first that we were meant to be together, and pushed through every barrier. Including my virginity.

He strokes my hair and tells me I'm doing so well for him. That I'm his good girl.

That doesn't make my body cooperate though.

"Breathe," he instructs me softly, and his hand lifts from my hair.

And I do.

"Look."

I open my eyes to find his pale-blue eyes full of love. Then I notice he's holding two fingers before my face. A second later, I see what he means.

"Your virgin blood, little bunny. The wolf got you." With slow deliberation he takes his fingers to his chest, and wipes bloody streaks across the top of his pectoral. "You're mine now, and I'm yours."

"Yes."

"In every way." He reaches back down between us and brings his fingers to his lips and crams them into his mouth, sucking my blood greedily as he holds my gaze, unblinking, like the predator he is. "I want every part of you."

He moves his hips, and I squeak in alarm or protest or surprise, I don't know which. He's huge inside me, and it stings. But there's also a spark of pleasure igniting in the place between my clit and where he has me speared.

"You're so tight, let me in further," he murmurs, tugging my hair slightly and magically, something shifts, like that releases the discomfort, and he's instantly deeper.

I can feel him all the way up to my heart. He's rearranging me internally with that big cock just as he's in my mind.

Then he thrusts.

My eyes roll back in my head, because Zane fucking me is like nothing I've ever felt before. It's a caress to parts of me that are untouched, and are so happy to be found by him, as though they've been waiting for Zane to light them up. He watches my expression intently as he repeats the motion, his muscles rippling. He's dragging out with teasing slowness then entering me faster each time. Each thrust is better as I open for him more.

"Oh fuck, Willow." His mouth opens and he's panting. He looks a bit crazed, and that's reassuring because so am I. "You're so wet, and feel so good. I can't wait to feel you come around my cock. I can't wait for this to be as good for you as it is for me."

"It is, it is," I babble. "I love you." I wrap my legs his hips to try to bring him closer.

"I love you too." He sounds on edge. "And you're my good girl. I want everyone to know you belong to *me*," he growls and even pushes deeper. "My ring on your finger, my child in your belly, my arm around your waist. The wolf isn't letting go of his prey this time."

20

ZANE

She's perfect.

I hold her hip down, and thrust harder into her. "You're not escaping again, you understand me?"

"Yes!" Willow's cunt grips me tighter, as though it's *me* that might escape. Ha. Not likely. I'd live in her like this if she let me. I can't ever get close enough.

"Mine." My voice sounds unhinged.

"I'm yours."

I'm an animal. I breathe in her neck, where the scent of strawberries is almost overpowered by the sweetness of her arousal. And I give in to what I've wanted to do since I saw her.

I bite her.

She cries out, but it's not intended to hurt. It's a suck that claims her just as I've claimed her pussy. I draw back to look, and there's my mark on her skin. A possessive growl escapes me.

"My beautiful good girl."

"Again." She turns her head, revealing the other side of her neck.

And that shocks me, even through the burning pleasure we're creating between us. I thought I'd have to apologise, but she's tilted her chin to give me better access.

I keep fucking into her wet, willing pussy, and the bliss is indescribable as I mark her again.

"Mine. Mine." I suck that soft, tender skin as I ram into her harder and harder. Her hips move with mine to get us together faster and deeper. My chest is bursting with love for this sweet girl who is so giving, who is allowing me to take everything I need from her.

And in return, I want to give her something special.

"Going to fill you up, little bunny," I grit out. "Pump you full of seed and make you pregnant."

"Please, yes," she gasps out.

We fit so easily together now, and her pussy is beginning to strangle my length as she winds up towards orgasm. This girl was made to take my cock, be spoiled by me, be mine to protect and adore.

I reach down, cramming my hand between us, until I find where her pearl is so close to where I'm slamming into her. She cries out the second I touch her, and I have to grit my teeth to prevent myself from shooting my load right then, too soon.

"Come for me. I need to feel you clench around my cock. Milk it out of me, little bunny." It's a harsh, guttural demand.

"Zane," she moans, and damn but I've needed that too. The sound of my name on her lips is magic.

"Come, and make me come inside you. You're going to make such cute babies. I'll give you as many as you want."

"Eight."

I choke a laugh.

She's beside herself. I won't take that as her real answer,

but if she wants? Sure. Eight miniature Willows? I should be knighted for providing the world with so much joy.

"I'll take you raw all the times it needs," I tell her, stroking her clit in time with my thrusts. "You'll never be without my come dripping down your thighs."

I'm losing control. My rhythm goes ragged. My balls pull up.

"Come." I'm the one gasping now. I can't hold on.

And good girl that she is, she does. Her first spasm sets me off, as her cry rings in my ears. I spray into her, shuddering. Then another pulse, and other. I empty myself into her as she grips my cock and holds me around the waist, her heels digging into my buttocks.

I must look like a monster, my face twisted in passion, but Willow keeps looking into my eyes like I'm hers and that's all that matters.

It takes long moments of us jerking together as we lose ourselves in our own pleasure and each other's, before we're motionless again. Still connected. Staring into her green eyes, for a second, I think we'll never separate again, and my heart is so content with that thought. I'm overcome by how good and right this is.

"I love you."

I can only drag in air and be so fucking grateful I found her in time, and carried her out of that church, until I recover enough of my brain to lift my weight from Willow before I crush her.

She makes a sound of dissent as I raise myself and reluctantly slip from the embrace of her welcoming pussy.

I untie her wrists then allow myself to collapse to the side, pulling Willow's hips stacked on top of mine, her shoulders still on the bed next to mine.

Turning my head towards her, I kiss her lips softly as I

cup her pussy, pushing the come that slipped momentarily out back where it belongs.

"Zane, that was…" She sounds exhausted. Wrecked.

"I know. I know." I slip my arm beneath her shoulders so her head flops on my bicep and cuddle her to me.

She wriggles a bit, and I clamp my other hand on her belly.

"Nope."

"No?" She stops moving. I feel her smile rather than see it, since my face is touching hers.

"I hope you're pregnant."

"Me too," she replies shyly.

"I want your sexy little bunny butt elevated every time we have sex until you have my first baby in you. Got to keep my come where it's required. I want you full, constantly. I want to be in your body and to consume your thoughts. Like you do mine." It's a bare declaration for all we've already said today.

"Pregnant the first time?" she asks.

"All your firsts," I remind her. I grin and her eyes go wide. "We're not done with that yet. And second, and third. All the times."

"Really?"

"Yes." And despite what I just said, I roll over her, then lean down and kiss her mouth. Not her first stolen kiss, nor the plundered second, or gifted third, but one of many. Infinite kisses.

"We'll never be finished with your firsts, little bunny," I whisper the truth against her lips. "I never intended to be."

21

WILLOW

7 MONTHS LATER

I reach up to the top shelf, and my body complains. Swollen ankles. Gah. But I manage to grasp the special edition book and pull it down.

"Ohhh..." The girl's eyes go wide as she accepts it.

"That's the one with the black pages, too," I tell her, and she gasps when she opens the hardback fantasy novel. Instead of black text on white, it's white text on black, and it looks amazing.

Stroking the pages reverently, my customer's eyes light up. "Thank you so much! I didn't think I'd be able to find a copy."

"You're welcome." I love to see that expression as someone finds just the right book. I remember how important books are and how losing yourself in a story can soothe any hurt.

I still read plenty, but it isn't the necessary escape that it used to be. Not since Zane kidnapped me and made me his.

The girl pays for her book, and while I wrap and bag it, her gaze flicks to the jar on the counter. "Is that fudge?"

I pass over her treasure with a smile. "Yep. Want a piece?"

"It does look delicious," she replies, which I take as a yes.

"It's my favourite." I open the jar and pull a piece of perfect, crumbly fudge and offer the open jar to the girl. I nibble the sweet treat, letting the creaminess melt in my mouth.

"That is divine," she says with a little moan that makes me chuckle.

"It is pretty amazing. My husband brought me that—full of vanilla fudge—on the day I opened the bookshop, and each week he visits to fill it up with a different flavour." I'd only mentioned in passing that I loved fudge, but nothing escapes Zane.

The girl puts her hand to her lips. "Really? That's so romantic!"

I nod, because she's right. Zane has taken time at every moment of our lives together to understand what I need and what I like, and to provide it. He knows everything about me, and he's as good as his word. When he caught me after our chase through the woods, he said he'd love me forever, and seven months later, we're more in love than we were on that first day.

He's been steadfast, and in return, I am joyous in my pursuit of all the things that make him happy. I'm still working on the perfect blowjob—though Zane says every single one is better than the last—and I hope I will find more and more ways to drive him wild for the rest of our lives.

Zane Bethnal. My wedding gate crasher, my kidnapper,

my husband. And now, my baby's daddy. I cup the underside of my bump and stroke the top.

"Thank you so much for the book." My customer peeks inside the paper bag and smiles again.

"Let me know if you like it. I'm always looking for new recs." Knowing what my customers enjoy is crucial, and personal recommendations are useful for ensuring I'm stocking what people in Bethnal, and those who visit from other parts of London, want to read. And even more important is selecting and sourcing the perfect book for the London Mafia Smut Club.

Honestly though, it's rarely a problem finding new favourites. One of the best bits of my job is the advance review copies. I get hardback editions or eBooks of my favourite authors' books weeks before release, and store all the pre-order copies carefully for my customers. And I have a precious copy for myself, to read while Zane plays with the kids, or in snatches of time while my assistant manages the shop.

"I will! Good luck with..." She nods awkwardly. "Everything."

I grin. "It's alright. Yes, I am pregnant. Twenty-eight weeks."

I'm carrying our first child, and even with the physical surprises like ankles the size of an elephant's and being rather front heavy, I'm so, so happy. Over the moon, and incredibly proud to have Zane's baby. He's given me everything I could want, and far, far more than I ever thought I'd have: love.

There isn't a day that goes past without Zane telling and showing me that he loves me in whispered words, possessive touches, or by making me lose my mind with pleasure.

"You're so lucky," she sighs, a look of longing taking over her face.

"You're single?" And it's a correct guess, because she nods.

"And that isn't going to change. I never get evenings off work. I'm a nanny," she explains.

No time off? "Your boss must be awful."

A dreamy expression floats onto her face. "He is. And he isn't."

"Well, keep the faith. You'll find someone, or they'll find you. Maybe when you don't expect it. That was certainly true for me."

"Maybe." And her voice is a bit sad.

"At least we have books," I say comfortingly. "Book boyfriends are the best boyfriends."

It isn't exactly a lie. How would I know about real boyfriends? I've only ever had my perfect husband, who—while he doesn't have bat wings—is everything I could wish.

"Men are better fictional, I guess." She fiddles with the handle of the carrier bag.

"You know, the next in the series will be released in the new year." I avoid answering. It's not nice to gloat that you're incandescently happily married. "Do you want me to pre-order it for you?"

She brightens. "Oh yeah! That would give me something to look forward to after Christmas. Yes, please. My name is Bella Harlow."

She gives me a London address in King's Cross, London, and I write it all down and make a mental note to ask Zane about the kingpin of that territory.

"Thanks! Happy Christmas!" Bella turns to the door with a cheery wave that seems forced.

"Hope you get what you want for Christmas!" I call after her.

She pauses. "Not much chance of that," she says, almost to herself, then pastes on a smile. "Cross your fingers for me, and I can't wait to see your baby when they arrive! I love babies."

"I will," I promise, then she's gone.

A tentative "Hi," turns my attention to my next customer. It's hours later when I've served dozens more people looking for Christmas gifts. I close the shop late because some browsers can't find the right thing, and I have to help them. But finally, I'm on my own in my dream bookstore.

When I first opened, I used to bring home a new book for Zane every day, at his insistence. He said he wanted to read all the books I'd read. He honestly prefers audiobooks though, and while he still asks for a weekly recommendation, I don't bring him paperbacks anymore. And it's fun to see him enjoying books he's picked for himself, too. I'm pretty sure he has the highest audio subscription tier, and buys extra credits.

It doesn't take long to deal with the money, and I'm finishing when the back of my neck prickles. I look up and see Zane in the doorway. He's let himself in with his key, and is leaning against the inner frame, his tall form imposing despite his relaxed pose. My heart patters, just as it did when I first saw him.

He's breathtakingly handsome, but instead of striding in to murder the man who would have kept me from him, he's smiling softly.

"What are you thinking about?" I ask, smiling back.

"Last night. Tonight. The rest of our lives," he replies in a low rasp that shivers up my spine.

I blush. Sex is different with a growing stomach, but I have to admit, from behind has advantages. And Zane is ravenous for my body—at least as much as usual, anyway—since I've been visibly pregnant.

He pushes off the door, hands still in his pockets and paces over to the counter where I'm sitting.

"Are you ready to go home, little bunny?" He phrases it as a gentle question, but I know it's nothing of the sort. It's a heated demand for my obedience.

Reaching for my coat and making my way to him, he takes it from my hands and holds it open for me to slide into. As he tucks it closed, he makes a rumbling sound in his chest like a big cat purring and strokes over my pregnant belly. "I'd love to bend you over that counter..."

"But you won't because you don't want me on my feet," I finish for him in a sing-song voice, rolling my eyes. If I had my way, he would. It's one of the many places Zane has taken me—frequently—but he won't anymore. For now.

"Nope." He shrugs in that arrogant way that I find hotter than I should. "You're taking such good care of my son, being a good girl for me and not overstraining yourself. So I get to look after *you*. And that means getting you home and putting your feet up. And then..."

"And then?" A frisson goes through me at his words.

His chuckle is downright wicked. "Ah, well. Once you're horizontal, that's different, isn't it? How are your cravings today? I was thinking we could make it the first time with chocolate..." He trails off and my imagination fills in delicious, filthy scenarios.

"Yes." There's never any other answer, except when it's that game we both enjoy, of him being my big bad. My kidnapper. My dark pursuer. My dangerous kingpin.

He tilts my chin up with his fingers to receive his kiss. "Did I ever tell you how bleak life was before I found you?"

I whimper as he kisses me softly and teasingly.

"I can't wait for us to have a child together." He says each word between kisses. "To help them grow up into murderous mafia bosses and bossettes—"

"Zane!" I splutter with laughter.

"Sorry." His voice is laced with amusement. "Law-abiding, successful bookshop owners." Another kiss, sweeter this time. "I'm looking forward to enjoying the gap between children when you can wear pretty summer dresses, and I'll rail you over this counter and dozens of other places. And to getting you pregnant again. To spending my life loving and protecting you and our kids."

"I love you so much." I don't have the words to express it like my husband does, but I feel it all the same.

"I fall in love with you more, every day." Sliding his big hand over my throat, he holds me gently there. Secure. He's got this power over me, but I trust him with anything. "Now, the wolf is going to take you home to *eat*, little bunny."

EPILOGUE
ZANE

7 Years later

The waves are really small at the beach today but that doesn't stop us from having fun. We have an inflatable unicorn that holds my two wriggling middle daughters. Caroline is splashing the water happily and Poppy is seemingly trying to drown the unicorn. Or perhaps give it a drink, I'm not entirely sure.

Our latest baby is on the sand with Willow, too small to join in the sea swimming. I sneak a glance over my shoulder at them, and under the umbrella on a big towel, Willow is blowing raspberries on Carl's tummy and a gooey feeling pools in my stomach. I love my family so much.

"Daddy," my eldest son calls out to me, pulling my attention back to the sea. He's on a violently-blue surfboard that's specially made for kids with soft edges. "Daddy, watch me surf this wave!"

The tiny bit of swell—no more than 3 inches—catches him paddling frantically, and he wobbles to his feet, standing for a good two seconds before he topples into the water.

"Whoop! That was a great ride!" I cheer as he emerges, grinning.

"I'm going to get the sea monster!" Olivia appears from nowhere—I'm not sure how that's possible in a pink swimming costume—and grabs my leg.

"Raahhh!" I make a generic monster noise and bear down on her, as a slight apology. I was totally distracted from the game we were playing, which was princesses vs sea monster.

But I commit.

Monster is a role I know well.

It's a long time later, when the princesses have defeated many reincarnations of the sea monster, the sea monster has capsized the great ship unicorn, numerous waves have been surfed, and everyone has wrinkled fingertips, that the kids are tired and hungry, and I shoo them up the beach to where Willow has a picnic ready.

Our eyes meet as I approach, and her gaze slides slowly down my body, lingering first over my heart on the tattoo of a willow tree and the wolf curled around a rabbit beneath it, then lower to where my board shorts are wet. I glance at them, and yeah, they're clinging. Enough for her to see the shape of my cock.

Witch. She knows her watching me like that will inevitably make me hard, and now is not the time. I shake the shorts out, but she merely redirects her gaze to the tattoos of our children's names that curl around my leg, just above my knee.

I give her a warning growl as I lean down and kiss her cheek.

"Don't start what you can't finish, little bunny," I rasp into her ear.

"Can't finish *right now*," she corrects me with a naughty smile. I ease down to sit on the towel next to her, then pull her onto my wet lap, and she shrieks.

"Ugh, they're so gross," Caroline grumbles, and the other kids agree. Even our youngest taps his spoon in disapproval.

I grin.

"This was your doing, Willow," I tell my wife, banding my arm around her waist to trap her to me. "You started it."

"Mmmm." She wriggles into me, and I hold her tight. "I did, didn't I?"

She lets out a contented sigh and we watch our kids eating happily on the beach in the sunshine for a second before I reluctantly let go to deal with our food and ensuring Poppy eats more than just chocolate for lunch. But not before I have a thought.

I need to wake earlier in the morning during this trip—before any of the kids—if I want quality time with their mother.

EXTENDED EPILOGUE
ZANE

7 Years later, the next morning

There's something special about waking up early, warm and comfortable in bed, anticipating the day ahead. My eyes pop open before the sun has risen, and my whole family is still asleep.

It's completely quiet. This trip to the coast has wiped everyone out.

Beside me, Willow is sleeping, her breath deep and even. She's wriggled away from me during the night, not always a snuggler, my girl. But that's okay. She makes up for it with her pre-sleep enthusiasm for being close to me, and knows I'll take what I want, when I need it, at night or any other time.

And while often the kids are awake before us, they aren't today. I'm going to take advantage.

I shift carefully, testing how asleep Willow is, then laugh to myself as she doesn't respond at all when I kiss her neck.

Out for the count.

Pushing the covers aside, I arrange her like she's my doll, on her back with her legs wide apart.

Dawn is beginning to break outside, the white light filtering in through the open curtains, as there's no one for miles around to look in.

I spit into my hand and admire my wife as I use the lubrication to stroke myself. Fuck, she's so pretty. Seven years since I saw her and *knew*, and every day I love and want her more. Her cunt is still slick and juicy from where I came inside her last night. I can never keep my hands off her.

Supporting myself on one arm, I spit on my palm again and cover the tip of my cock before sliding the head over her open pink slit.

She's so beautiful there. Not the virgin little cunt I had the first time, but more welcoming, always wet for me, and perfectly tight. Especially when we play this game.

I hold myself at her entrance and slowly push the first inch into her, biting back a groan at how good she feels, while simultaneously trying not to wake her. She grips me with her little pussy, and fuck, she's amazing. I alternate looking at where I'm breaching her, and checking her lovely, peaceful face.

I stroke up and down my exposed shaft, wondering about making myself come here, relishing how illicit this is.

Just the tip.

No need to drug her to indulge my darkest fantasies. All Willow needs is a day at the beach and she's dead to the world. It's perverted, but I love using her like this, anticipating the moment she wakes and sees me. It's a race whether I can get both of us to come before she opens her eyes.

So yeah, the reason early mornings are so special to me

has nothing to do with the gorgeous sunrise over the sea, and everything to do with possessing my wife in every hour of the day and night. I push deeper, and the feel of her tight passage lubricated with my come makes me horny as if I was twenty-seven like she is. I will never get enough of her. Willow is my world.

I withdraw and thrust down further, and a grunt escapes me as she eases open and lets me in. I'm convinced that I've lost the game, and stop moving, my gaze held by her face. She's going to catch me if I plunge into her again.

Surely?

But no. She shifts slightly, but slumbers on.

I take more, and she gives, letting me in more and more until I'm fully over her, hips pistoning, my balls slapping on her arse.

There's not a moment I don't want her. Really, it's considerate not to wake her with my savage desires.

"I love you, little bunny." I whisper the words.

"Zane." She mumbles in her sleep, squirming on my cock, her eyes still closed.

I reach down, cramming my hand between our bodies, and stroke her clit. She opens her mouth in a wordless plea, almost panting.

"That's it, come for me. Come for the man who had to have you, whatever the cost."

Harder and harder, I thrust into her, rubbing her clit. The savage pleasure of this is wrong, and yet, I'm winning at our game and having Willow exactly as I need, so I don't care.

I take more. And more. I'm ramming into my wife's wet but unwitting pussy... until her eyes fly open, and she looks straight at me. And breaks.

"*Zane.*" Willow cries out my name as she clenches

around me in wave after wave. I keep going while she tries to milk me.

"You feel so good," I grit out. "My good fucking girl. Such a good girl for your obsessed husband."

She must be partly in shock—it still surprises her sometimes the depth of my need for her—because she doesn't reply. Instead, she alternately sucks in air, and smiles, and blinks her eyes long like a contented cat.

It's tempting to come inside her again, but I did that last night, and now she's awake, I have a filthier target in mind. I pull out and fist around my length, brutally hard.

I pump up and down once, twice, three times, and then the pleasure overtakes me. I come, spurting it all over her belly and tits.

I cover her with it. And fuck, but it's primal. It's ownership. It's putting my DNA on her, just like I put it in her. It's hot and possessive.

As the ecstasy ebbs away it's me that's shaken.

Because my sweet, innocent wife is running her finger through the white seed I've sprayed over her soft belly, and licking it from the tip like it's icing on her favourite lemon drizzle cake.

"Good morning, husband," she says with a naughty grin.

I'm shattered from my orgasm, but I can't help but return her smile. "Wife. I see you're helping yourself to breakfast."

"Good of you to provide it for me in bed. Hard working, aren't you?" She takes another lick, this time obscenely pressing her finger in her mouth.

Impossibly, my cock twitches with interest.

"I aim to please," I murmur.

"This won't give me that baby you promised me."

Raising one eyebrow, I lean down to claim a morning kiss, deep and slow and sexy.

"I won, Zane." She shudders as I kiss down her neck.

"Yep." I suck at the tender skin hard enough to leave a subtle mark. One that's longer lasting. "My clever little bunny."

I was fucking her *hard*. We need more beach days, and my wife needs more sleep. Then maybe the next baby should be by stealth.

"And now you need to give me something delicious to eat," I say between kisses as I begin to make my way further. "One more orgasm, this time as I lick you. Before the kids wake up."

THANKS

Thank you for reading, I hope you enjoyed it.

Want to read a little more Happily Ever After? Click to get exclusive epilogues and free stories! or head to EvieRoseAuthor.com

If you have a moment, I'd really appreciate a review wherever you like to talk about books. Reviews, however brief, help readers find stories they'll love.

Love to get the news first? Follow me on your favored social media platform - I love to chat to readers and you get all the latest gossip.

If the newsletter is too much like commitment, I recommend following me on BookBub, where you'll just get new release notifications and deals.

- amazon.com/author/evierose
- bookbub.com/authors/evie-rose
- instagram.com/evieroseauthor
- tiktok.com/@EvieRoseAuthor

INSTALOVE BY EVIE ROSE

Accidentally Kidnapping the Mafia Boss

I might have kidnapped him, but the mafia boss isn't going to let me go.

Grumpy Bosses

Older Hotter Grumpier

My billionaire boss catches me reading when I should be working. And the punishment…?

Tall, Dark, and Grumpy

When my boss comes to fetch me from a bar, I'm expecting him to go nuts that I'm drunk and described my fake boyfriend just like him. But he demands marriage…

Silver Fox Grump

He was my teacher, and my first off-limits crush. Now he's my stalker, and my boss.

Stalker Kingpins

Spoiled by my Stalker

From the moment we lock eyes, I'm his lucky girl… But there's a price to pay

Kingpin's Baby

I beg the Kingpin for help… And he offers marriage.

Owned by her Enemy

I didn't expect the ruthless new kingpin—an older man, gorgeous and hard—to extract such a price for a ceasefire: an arranged marriage.

His Public Claim

My first time is sold to my brother's best friend

Pregnant by the Mafia Boss

Baby Proposal

My boss walked in on me buying "magic juice" online... And now he's demanding to be my baby's daddy!

Groom Gamble

I accidentally gave my hot boss my list of requirements for a perfect husband: tall, gray eyes, nice smile, big d*ck. High sperm count.

Kingpin's Nanny

My grumpy boss bought my whole evening as a camgirl!

London Mafia Bosses

Captured by the Mafia Boss

I might be an innocent runaway, but I'm at my friend's funeral to avenge her murder by the mafia boss: King.

Taken by the Kingpin

Tall, dark, older and dangerous, I shouldn't want him.

Stolen by the Mafia King

I didn't know he has been watching me all this time.

I had a plan to escape. Everything is going perfectly at my wedding rehearsal dinner until *he* turns up.

Caught by the Kingpin

The kingpin growls a warning that I shouldn't try his patience by attempting to escape.

There's no way I'm staying as his little prisoner.

Claimed by the Mobster

I'm in love with my ex-boyfriend's dad: a dangerous and powerful mafia boss twice my age.

Snatched by the Bratva

I have an excruciating crush on this man who comes into the coffee shop. Every day. He's older, gorgeous, perfectly dressed. He has a Russian accent and silver eyes.

Kidnapped by the Mafia Boss

I locked myself in the bathroom when my date pulled out a knife. Then a tall dark rescuer crashed through the door... and kidnapped me.

Held by the Bratva

"Who hurt you?"

Before I know it, my gorgeous neighbour has scooped me up into his arms and taken me to his penthouse. And he won't let me go.

Seized by the Mafia King

I'm kidnapped from my wedding

Abducted by the Mafia Don

"Touch her and die."

Filthy Scottish Kingpins

Forbidden Appeal

He's older and rich, and my teenage crush re-surfaces as I beg the former kingpin to help me escape a mafia arranged marriage. He stares at me like I'm a temptress he wants to banish, but we're snowed in at his Scottish castle.

Captive Desires

I was sent to kill him, but he's captured me, and I'm at his mercy. He says he'll let me go if I beg him to take his...

Eager Housewife

Her best friend's dad is advertising for a free use convenient housewife, and she's the perfect applicant.